C000124708

Jade Fish
and the Master

A trilogy

Paddy Salmon

Jade Fish and the Master's series

Following the «Tao Té Ching» of Lao Tzu.
Each volume is in 81 Sections in 9 Parts, or chapters.

BOOK ONE
- **Jade Fish and the Master - 'Fu' The Turning Point.**
  Is the first in the series called «Jade Fish and the Master».

THIS BOOK TWO
- **Jade Fish and the Qin - 'Ming I' The Darkening of the Light.**

BOOK THREE
- **Jade Fish and the Tao - 'Wei Chi' Before Completion.**
  This is the concluding volume in the series.

9or/£2.50
uk6

Paddy Salmon

Jade Fish and the Master

Book One

'Fu' – The Turning Point

Map of the Eastern Zhou Empire
C.280 BCE

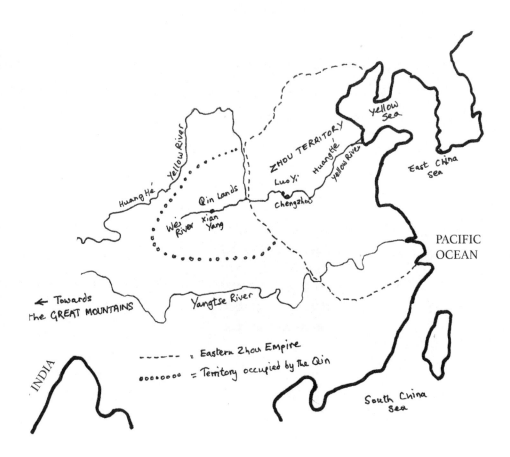

For our four grandchildren,
Ezekiel, Felix, Louis and Elias

© Paddy Salmon 2023

Map of Jade Fish's Journey

- - - - - = Route taken by Lao Tzu & Jade Fish

✗ ✗ ✗ ✗ Frontier of Zhou Dynasty

City of Peacocks
KŎNQUÉ CHENG

Road to cheng-zhou the Zhou capital

River of the North

ZHOU TERRITORY

Lake of Paradise

LANDS OF THE QIN

Jade cutter's House

SNOW PEAKS MOUNTAINS

Wise Woman

Cave

Volcano

Shepherds

Road Leading to X'ian Yang, the Qin capital

Biāncheng Border Town

← To THE GREAT MOUNTAINS

YELLOW RIVER

QIN TERRITORY

PART ONE

The Tao (or Way) that can be spoken of is not the true Tao.
The names that can be named out loud are not the eternal names.
It was from the nameless that heaven and earth had their origins...

(**Tao Tê Ching** - The Classic of the Way and Its Virtue - I)

I   Once, when the world was greener, an orange sun nearly two and a half thousand years younger than it is now was setting as usual. It dipped slowly beyond the watchtowers of a remote border town in a western province of the Zhou Empire, far away from the regal courts of Chéng-zhōu, which had become the imperial capital in the east.

Not far from the town centre was a large compound made up of paved courtyards and blossoming gardens. There, several huts and small houses seemed to kneel at the foot of a particularly beautiful palace of fretted timbers and storeys piled like a tiered wedding cake. It had white colonnades, broad verandas and enamelled red-tiled roofs, curling up at the ends. The roofs and all of the dark windows seemed to stare down disdainfully over the heads of the other lowlier dwellings.

In a garden of this mansion, which belonged to the Border Magistrate, a young girl called Jade Fish was busy washing a large and highly decorated red-enamelled vase. She was sitting on the low, white marble parapet of one of the many fountains in the garden, with her bare feet deliciously cool in the water while she worked. She sang to the painted animals on the priceless vessel as she rinsed it out with clean water and let the fountain play over its embossed pictures and patterns. The glossy pitcher was heavy and nearly as big as the girl. Nearby a white peacock screamed suddenly in anguish, almost as if it knew what would happen next.

2   In the main square of the town, the noises of the market had subsided. There were smells of fish grilling, onions frying and soup pots steaming with chopped ginger, little cucumbers, peppers and coriander leaves. Chicken pieces were spitting crisply over darkly reddened beds of charcoal. These scents all came drifting with the blue smoke in the warm breeze. Gongs clanged from a temple somewhere. A helmeted guard clad all in dark-green leather armour spat towards the red terra-cotta dust of the street and hitched his sword belt higher round his waist, swapping a joke as he did so with a man holding the reins of a little donkey cart. Behind the driver's bench of rust coloured planks the cart was heavily laden with long lime-green bamboo staves. A few sheep bleated, as they were urged and pushed on their way by an elderly shepherd. He apologised to the passers-by who had to make way for them.

All was as peaceful as you would have expected under a Zhou queen and her royal consort, even though the lands that would later become China were living through a time we know now as the Period of the Warring States.

3   Up on the city walls, high above the market place was a square, stone tower with crenelated turrets. This was the Gatekeeper's post with a view out across the wide river beyond the walls he guarded. From there he could see the river currents drifting alongside the walls for a while and then parting company with them to aim for the southern plains. The mountains in the far west, where the sun was lowering itself gently, were small in the distance. Their smoky, prussian-blue silhouettes sharply broke the gilded line of the horizon to the west. These formed part of the forbidden lands of the Qin, and beyond them lay the lofty wildernesses of what is now known as Tibet. From them this famed river had tumbled in its youth and behind them the sun was now sinking below their darkly jagged outlines. The Gatekeeper watched as two white cranes soared above the river heading north.

Inside the tower was a steeply winding stone stairway that led down to the streets. The Gatekeeper would descend them once the sun had performed its daily trick of magic and disappeared under the distant line of hills. The heavy, iron-studded gates of the town would then be barred shut until they were reopened in the early morning. Those Qin merchants with authorisations could pass in from the forbidden west to trade during the day, but nobody from the eastern side was allowed to pass the other way, either by day or by night. Overseeing the closing of the Western Gates and supervising all authorisations was the Gatekeeper's task each day.

The Gatekeeper was a tall man with watchful eyes. Though elderly, he was fit and strong. His thick and straggling, grey moustaches made up for the lack of hair on his bald head. That day he was staring down at the market place as he did every evening before he shut the great gates. Like the guard below he too had a green leather helmet and the same dark-green leather armour that marked him out as a Border Guard. He reached for his helmet and started buckling it on.

"Will it be today?" he said out loud to himself for perhaps the ninth time that afternoon. "I have seen only white sheep all day. He will surely not come today. Perhaps he will never come! Maybe it has all been an elaborate trick."

The sun had gone. There was only a pink and purple absence below the green evening sky to the west.

"He will not come now, surely?" the man muttered. "It is too late. I hear the gates closing. I must go down to check that the servants are locking them properly. Perhaps he will come tomorrow instead."

4   But the man's attention was suddenly drawn to the far end of the market square where a boy was tugging at a fat black sheep with a large bronze bell under its chin. The sheep was reluctant to move and the boy had to pull hard, shouting, to get the animal to advance. The clanging of the bell and the bleated protests seemed to be in competition with each other.

"Surely," muttered the Gatekeeper, taking his iron bar with him as he hurried down the steps, "surely it cannot be the sign I have been waiting to discover for so long. Three months I have expected this, and it's now three years since I was first contacted."

Reaching the base of the walls, the tall man hurried over to the boy with the black sheep. The animal jerked backwards in great alarm.

"Where are you taking that fine black sheep?" he asked the boy who had been peering all over the market place. "Have you a message from your master?"

The boy turned his head to stare up at this tall man.

"Are you the Gatekeeper?" he said. "My master told me to make sure I gave this sheep to the Gatekeeper. You look much too tall to be a Gatekeeper."

"Of course I am the Gatekeeper! What nonsense! Come with me and you shall see me as we lock the Western Gates. Are you new here? Have you not seen me before?"

The boy shook his head.

"I am from the east," he said. "My master said to tell you he should be here shortly."

5   At that moment the peace of the evening was broken by a screeching and yelling in the distance. All heads turned towards the eastern side of the market place, where the sky was darkening to a deep indigo. Were they shouts of fear? Screams of anger?

A young girl entered the huge square, running silently as if her life depended on it, turning her head to glance behind her as she raced on bare feet across the sand. Chasing after her was a line of noisy pursuers: women, men, and some older children, twenty or thirty in all and gaining on the girl. Shaking their fists and shouting wildly at her they drew closer and closer. Finally, as she turned her head desperately once more to see where they were, the young girl tripped over an iron cooking pot and fell sprawling in the reddish dust, landing at the feet of the handsome black sheep, the open-mouthed boy and the tall Gatekeeper in his green leather uniform. She lay there panting desperately and rubbing her left knee, which was bleeding.

The shouting behind her subsided and the crowd gathered in a circle round her.

6   The Gatekeeper leaned down and helped the girl to her feet. Of medium height, she looked about thirteen years old, with unusual green, almond-shaped eyes that glowered defiantly at her pursuers. She wore dark grey cotton trousers and a faded blue velvet jerkin. Around her thin neck was a leather cord holding a curious fish that was beautifully carved out of pale green jade.

"What is the matter here?" said the Gatekeeper in a different tone of voice from the one he had used to the boy. This was his Voice of Authority. Although he was not one of the Imperial Guards, he was nevertheless in the armed service of Zhou Ting and had the post of Keeper of the Western Gates. A significant position indeed!

A woman in a blue silk suit stepped forward looking very angry indeed. Her black hair was elegantly arranged with a comb made of tortoise shell stuck at the back. She wore so much gold and silver on her arms and around her neck that she jangled when she moved.

"I am Ning Mei, the Wife of the Magistrate," said the woman coldly. "This Kitchen Girl broke our best porcelain vase. Clumsy girl! It isn't the first time she has been so thoughtless. She's broken valuable things before. She must be punished and then given more work. That will stop her dreaming!"

"Oh, please, sir! It wasn't like that at all. Her son came past and pushed me, deliberately. You ask him!"

The girl turned round and pointed accusingly at a plump boy in a brilliant silk suit of yellow and pale blue. The boy's eyes seemed to grow round with disbelief and he smiled sleekly at her.

"I never went near her. Why should I? The Kitchen Girl isn't somebody I'd want to speak to, let alone touch!"

"You see," said his mother haughtily. "Go straight back to the palace kitchens, girl! The servants have orders to beat you. Then you can begin to make amends by chopping all the wood for the next ten days, on top of your other kitchen duties."

"I shall not go back!" cried the girl wildly. "I'm falsely accused and you are all so horrible to me! I shall leave tonight!"

At this there was much laughter and jeering amongst the small crowd who were gathered around this scene.

"Hah! Where would a young girl go on her own?" "The Kitchen Girl cannot just leave the Magistrate's household!" "The family *owns* her. How can she leave? What a joke!"

"I would just as soon get rid of you, surely," spat the fine lady coldly, "but you would have nowhere to go, and anyway, you're part of my Household."

7   Just then, there was a deep but polite cough, somewhat like a large dragon gently clearing its throat.

At the same instant, all eyes noticed that a newcomer had appeared, as if from out of the ground, and was standing behind the Gatekeeper and the boy with the black sheep. He was a large giant of a man, as wide and rugged as an old oak tree, with a great burly head and the most enormous ears that you had ever seen. Dense white moustaches framed his thick, dark lips and dangled to well below his several chins. His eyes twinkled and seemed to peep through the folds of flesh on his wrinkled face, as if they were constantly laughing.

"What claim do you have on this girl, may I ask?" growled the massive newcomer pleasantly, smiling as he did so at the lady. "You are the Magistrate's Wife? You surely don't need her that much. A woman like you would have many servant girls, isn't that so?"

His eyes beamed with amusement, though it was not clear what he found so humorous.

"She's not a slave, if that's what you mean," said the woman contemptuously. "I do not care where she goes, though she has broken my most precious vase. I am owed *that* in value."

"Vases may break," said the strange old man, nodding his great head. "A woman of your position will have many others. Let me take this poor girl off you, for she'll only break more vases and cause you more anguish."

"What does the girl say?" said the woman in her icy tones. "Do you want to go with this... this elderly stranger? He'll probably end up beating you far more than I ever shall. Go, if you wish it. But I shall never have you back again if you dare to leave my Household."

There was a pause and people craned forward so they could catch the girl's response.

"Yes, I *shall* go with this man!" said the girl defiantly, raising her chin. "I never want to see any of you again, as long as I live!"

Saying this, she strode across and stood next to the corpulent giant. Behind him was a massive black water buffalo with long, waxy-white horns. A rope led from the buffalo's thick neck to the large hands of the whiskery colossus with the enormous ears and the mild eyes.

"So be it!" declared the Magistrate's Wife magisterially, turning away as if to brush the spectacle from her mind.

"Who is he?" whispered many voices around the circle. "Who can such a man be?"

"Master," declared the Gatekeeper, finally turning to him, "I've waited many months for this moment. So, you have finally arrived!"

"And I appear to have gained a dependant," sighed the vast and ancient-looking stranger, seemingly to himself. "Just when I thought I was turning at last to peace and solitude."

"It is too late to pass through the gates today, Master," whispered the Gatekeeper privately to the extraordinary newcomer. "You will please stay this night at my home, which is nearby. My wife will feed us all and there's room to sleep. And room also for your water buffalo. Excuse me a minute while I check on the Gates."

"You may go, child," said the massive old man to the boy with the black sheep. "Make sure you feed her well before you sell her at the market tomorrow. You may keep the proceeds."

The boy bowed, his eyes shining with pleasure, and he disappeared with the handsome black beast.

The crowd slowly dispersed, for the fun was clearly over. The Magistrate's wife and her followers were marching aloofly back towards the ornate palace with the green verandas and the dark, red-tiled roofs.

"Come, now," said the gigantic fellow in a kindly fashion to the girl. "You made a brave decision this evening, my dear. But I have no idea what to do with you. You will have to put up with me for a while. What do you think of that?" His eyes shone with amusement. "I might be a dreadful ogre, for all you know."

"From the bottom of my heart I thank you, sir," replied the girl gratefully, pressing her two slim hands together and bowing low. "I was pushed and I have never been treated well at the Magistrate's house. I shall be honoured to serve you, even if you are an ogre. I don't know what ogres are like. May I, too, call you Master? I don't know who you are. Who *are* you?"

"Who *am* I? Hah! What man can ever hope to answer *that* question?" answered the stranger, his huge belly wobbling with laughter that sounded like distant thunder rolling over loosely tiled roof tops. "Who do *you* suppose me to be, Gatekeeper?"

"Master," answered the tall Palace Guard, who had by now returned from checking the Gates. "I know that you were Keeper of the Archives in the Imperial Courts of Chéng-zhōu. And I know, too, that you sent me word that you wanted to pass through the Gates to travel to the western wilderness, something which of course is forbidden. I know also that you are working on..."

"Working on my final labour, whatever that may be," interrupted the enormous old man. He laughed softly again, this time a great rumbling chuckle, like unwanted buildings crumbling and tumbling down into the dirt. "Where on earth should I keep it? A lifetime spent working on dusty documents and now I have one last project, do I? Wouldn't I need a palace to store all my notes?"

"Is this all you have?" asked the Gatekeeper surprised. "One buffalo and a few bags on its back? But where are all your documents, Master?"

"Gathering yet more dust in the Emperor's library, my friend. All that I need nowadays I carry in my head, as I have always done. Come, I'm hungry for your good wife's soup, and so is this poor girl. Child, I know the Gatekeeper's name is Yin Hsi, and I am Lao Tzu, but what do they call you, young lady?"

"Jade Fish is the name I am called, Master, or Yu Yù," answered the girl shyly, holding up the quaintly carved green jade fish that hung around her thin neck. "I have no other names, as far as I know, sir."

8   "Jade Fish?" murmured the huge man softly, as if to himself. "Yu Yù? Well, well!"

Dusk had by now given way to night as swiftly as it always did in these parts. Now the market place was alight: little red lanterns with silk or paper shades hung in the trees or on poles near the stalls; small charcoal fires glowed where street vendors cried their wares and handed out steaming bowls or hot delicacies wrapped in large leaves. Crickets were rasping out their harsh chirruping in the darkened gardens and leafy courtyards of the homes situated around the market square.

Leading the Water Buffalo, who answered to the name of Shuïniù, the three of them walked to a small house just behind the square. Viewed from behind, their dark silhouettes looked incongruous. One was of medium height and slender, one was stringy and tall, like a beanpole, and the third was simply massive. The Gatekeeper's house was painted white and was set in a garden of magnolia trees, whose large white flowers glowed in the light from the lanterns strung along the veranda in front of the wooden single-storey house.

The Gatekeeper's wife, Yin Nuan, was a warm and homely woman with a welcoming smile for her guests. She busied herself building up her kitchen fire and adding food to the iron cauldron fixed on an iron hook above the charcoals. Sweet smells of fish and vegetables drifted round the small courtyard. Bed rolls were found and unrolled. She and Jade Fish talked quietly while the food was being prepared. The two men sat peacefully sipping tea while the crickets continued to serenade them with their raucous music.

9 "I shall have to look after this girl," said the gigantic old man reflectively, tugging at one of his enormous ears. "I cannot leave until her future has been settled. She is my responsibility now. I never had a daughter, you know. Son, yes, but not a daughter."

"Our daughter is settled in the east, Master," said the Gatekeeper. "We live on our own now, my wife and I. The girl may stay here with us, if you wish. We could look after her."

"That is kind and considerate of you, Gatekeeper, but it would not be true to the Way," said the Master. "The Tao requires hidden things to be shown and this girl clearly needs my help to find her own Way in this world."

He turned to the girl who was staring up at him wide-eyed with wonder.

"A great journey, my dear, starts with a small footstep. I have my own journey to make in due course, but I shall help you with yours if you wish it. Where do you come from and where do you wish to go?"

"I don't know where I come from," she answered, "and therefore I have little idea where I want to go. I'd like to know where I was born and who my parents are."

"A reasonable request surely, don't you think, Gatekeeper?" laughed the huge man.

"I have only three things I really wish to teach, you know," he continued, turning back to the girl. "They are simplicity, patience and compassion. These three virtues are our greatest treasures and I too must constantly relearn and rehearse them."

"But, Master, what of your journey and your great work?" asked the Gatekeeper.

"My journey started a long time ago," came the calm answer, "and my work is nearly all done. I have only to copy it out before I leave you. You may look after it, then, and see that it's available for those who might wish to study it. Meanwhile, we shall try to help the girl to find her Way. As always, however, we shall practise the art of *Wu Wei*."

The old man smiled and raised a cup of tea to his lips. He drank appreciatively.

Before he could be questioned further the fish soup arrived, along with flat breads newly baked on the coals, and soon there was relaxed talk, as the four people, strangers no more, ate together and laughingly told each other their stories. The only complaints came, loudly, from the frogs who were socialising in the pond at the back of the house. They barked and quacked at each other and seemed to have so much to protest about.

But finally, the frogs like everybody else settled and stilled. The whole town was hushed. The stars above held their sway and the moon was just another silvery lantern, set high amidst the magnolia flowers in the blue darkness of just another night.

The nameless and the named both have their origins in darkness.
There is a darkness within darkness
And that is the gateway to eternal mystery.

(**Tao Tê Ching** - The Classic of the Way and Its Virtue I)

PART TWO

Something was strangely formed
That existed before earth and heaven were conceived:
In silence and emptiness,
Self-sufficient and unchanging,
Ever present and unfailing,
Maybe the Mother of all things.
We don't know its real name,
So it goes by the name of Tao:
The great Tao.
It flows far and wide
And having gone away,
It returns....

(**Tao Tê Ching** - The Classic of the Way and its Virtue XXV)

I   The early morning was chilly with a dewy sheet of minute pearls that covered the grass and flowers of the garden. In the half-light of the dawn the old man rose to perform his exercises. Though he was vast in size, his movements were surprisingly agile and graceful. He stood still and faced the grey east where the sun would show itself a little later. A solitary mynah bird whistled softly from its perch high in the trees.

The Master's arms rose and fell, gently and slowly, in time

with his breathing. He crouched and took steps, this way and that way, while his weight transferred itself easily from foot to foot. Yin and yang. Lightness and weight. Pushing and parrying. Lowering and lifting.

As he was Embracing the Tiger and Returning It to the Mountain (or *Pao Hu Kwei Shan*), he became aware of the girl. She had quietly taken up a position behind him. She watched him closely. Then she too moved, lightly and carefully, copying his unhurried gestures and footsteps. The flowing movements were slow and delicate, and the breathing that accompanied them was regular: in and out, with the same easy grace. There was a rooted balance and a soft steeliness in the dance-like sequence.

Outside the garden, the world had begun to awaken and the sun prepared to hoist itself again above the horizon of the east. It would soon be poised like a crimson ball over the lands where Zhou emperors presently ruled in ornate, eastern palaces. The Gatekeeper had already left to oversee the opening of the great, carved Town Gates.

Inside the garden, the Master's slow parries and deep punches continued without a pause. The girl's light kicks and delicate steps mirrored the old man's unhurried movements, in harmony until the end. They had Waved Hands like Clouds or *Yun Shou*, the Fair Maiden had Worked at the Shuttles, or *Yu Nu Ch'uan Shu*, and the Tiger's Ears had been Held, or *Ta Hu*.

Now, after the Grand Terminus, or *He T'ai Chi*, there was peace and the silence held just their gentle breathing.

2   "Master," said the Gatekeeper as they sat on cushions on the floor, eating rice with vegetables and sipping a chicken broth made with ginger, sweet peppers and cardamoms, "please explain to me what you meant by *Wu Wei* yesterday. Should we not try hard to achieve certain things in our lives?"

The old man laughed softly, a great, cavernous and happy grumbling from deep in his enormous belly.

"Too many people are trying too hard for too many things. If, however, you follow the path of *Wu Wei*, you will listen rather than speak. You will learn to be still long before you move. You will learn plenty from water, that most mysterious of all the elements around us. In this world, Yin Hsi, there is nothing more submissive and weak than water; yet for attacking something that's strong and unyielding, nothing can be more powerful or more terrible than water. *Wu Wei* achieves without effort."

"I've spoken with my wife," said Yin Hsi, the Gatekeeper. "My brother-in-law will look after the Gates until I return. May I come with you, Master?"

"How can I stop you?" said Lao Tzu, his moustaches twitching with laughter and his eyes full of merriment. "I have no idea, Gatekeeper, what we shall do or where we shall go, but we must find this girl's Way with her, and it may be that we shall discover our own Way at the same time."

Yin Hsi's wife, Yin Nuan, was soon clucking her teeth softly as she prepared clothing and bedrolls along with some supplies of rice and tea. These were packed into the brown leather saddlebags slung over the Water Buffalo. Yin Nuan carefully attached the bags with thick canvas straps that were buckled under Shuïniù's wide black belly.

Shuïniù's big mournful eyes were torn between staring at the people and gazing at the bundles of hay laid out for her breakfast.

3 "I was told by the shepherd couple who adopted me that they found me in the mount-ains," Jade Fish had told everyone over supper the previous evening.

"The shepherds who lived up in the hills beyond here raised me. They had been unhappy because they had no children of their own, so they were very pleased to look after me. They told me I wasn't their daughter but they treated me just as if I were their child. I liked them very much indeed and they were good to me. They always showed me plenty of love."

"That's good," Lao Tzu had commented. "All babies and children need to be held closely and talked with continually. They learn from us and we can learn from them. You cannot give small children too much affection."

"One day, however," continued the girl, "when I was nine years old, they said I had no future with an old couple like them. They didn't want to give me up, but they thought I would do better if I served in the Magistrate's household in the Border Town. They said I would have a more promising future. I was very sad to leave them."

"Did the Magistrate treat you so badly?" asked Yin Hsi. "He's not thought to be a bad person in the town."

"No, sir," replied the girl. "I think I learned more from the Magistrate than from anybody else, for I used to run away in my few, spare moments and creep into the back of his Court to watch and listen to the legal cases that he was hearing. I found all of that fascinating. No, it was his wife and the rest of the family who were harsh and unfair to me."

"Would you know the shepherds' home again if you saw it?" Lao Tzu asked.

"I think I'd recognise their village and their house, Master," Jade Fish had replied. "It was over the hills, going north and east."

Now, as the sun rose, they said their goodbyes to Yin Nuan and set out on the road. The Water Buffalo seemed to know the way so they followed in her footsteps. Shuïniù had beautiful horns, wrinkled and shiny like ancient ivory, crusted and polished with age. The horns swept out in great bows and curved upwards. The girl had asked Yin Nuan the Gatekeeper's wife if she could tie coloured ribbons and brass bells to the horns, so before they left that is what she and Yin Nuan did together.

They stopped at a wide river before the track began to climb amongst the hills to the north. The Water Buffalo was very happy to find water at last. They unstrapped the bags, removed the ribbons and bells and let her wallow in the sandy shallows. Jade Fish wandered a little way along the path leading upstream while the two men brewed tea in the shade of some jade-green weeping willows. As they talked quietly and sipped tea they watched the girl carefully to make sure no harm would come to her.

Jade Fish delicately and quietly eased herself into the river. Her cotton clothes were soon soaked, but it was a warm day and they would dry quickly on her. The water came up well above her knees. She bent down and held her right hand motionless under the water. After ten minutes, during which the girl stood without moving a muscle, a fat trout came swimming silkily upstream. It nibbled at the streaming weeds that swirled below the surface, waving its tail while its head stayed perfectly still. Finally, the fish cautiously edged forward and paused over her hand, as if reflecting.

Gently, Jade Fish began to tickle the belly of the fish. The silvery body of the fish relaxed and became almost as immobile as the girl's. Only its tail still waved slowly in the current. The girl's fingers continued to tickle and stroke the soft stomach of the mesmerised trout.

Suddenly, Jade Fish's hand came shooting up with a loud splash and the fish was hurtled into the air to land on the bank. There it flapped and squirmed in startled surprise. The girl took a flat stick she had found near the trees and whacked the fish sharply on the head until its body went limp. The two men sipped their tea and watched.

The girl repeated the trick a second and then a third time. In less than an hour she had caught three plump fish, and she proudly laid them on the grass before the two men.

"The shepherd showed me how to do that," she said. "Now we have our evening meal."

The men laughed and applauded her.

"Well, Master," said Yin Hsi, grinning, "was the girl practising *Wu Wei* there? Did she not try to catch those fish?"

Lao Tzu smilingly replied, "I think they just came to her naturally, Gatekeeper. She and the fish were in harmony with the element of water, but it's in the nature of humans to want to eat fish, just as it's in the nature of fish to make it difficult to let themselves be caught."

4   It was late in the warm afternoon of the third day when Jade Fish looked about her as they climbed up a hillside.

"I think I remember these hills," she said, shading her eyes. "We used to come to a market each week in that village down there."

She pointed to a group of huts and homesteads in the distance at the end of a wide valley.

"We must climb over that hill to the north and then, I think, we'll find the sheep and the shepherds."

The way was steep and the Gatekeeper found that he was puffing as he climbed. The Water Buffalo also found it an effort to heave her great frame up the track. But the great-bellied old man and the slender young girl both climbed effortlessly, picking their way nimbly amongst the rocks and crevices like mountain goats.

At the top they paused to look at the view. Lines of hills to the north faded into the pale distance, becoming bluer even than the sky. Mountains still further away rose to crests that had the brilliance of snow upon them. And on the other side of their own ridge there were flocks of sheep grazing peacefully. In the valley below, mere dots seen from this height, were several wooden huts belonging to shepherds.

In one of these Jade Fish finally found the elderly shepherd couple who had adopted her. They had lined, weather-beaten faces and were dressed in simple lambskin robes. The elderly man stood near the door leaning on his long crook and keeping an eye out for his sheep. His wife was busy feeding a young lamb with milk from a leather bottle with a wooden teat at the end. She looked tired and care-worn, but the minute she saw the girl, she dropped the poor lamb and the bottle in her haste to take the girl in her arms, laughing and crying in her excitement. Both she and her husband were overjoyed to see Jade Fish again and they hugged and kissed the girl in turn, almost unable to let her go. Introducing her fellow travellers, Jade Fish explained why they had come to see the couple, and the two old shepherds said that they would tell their guests all they knew over supper. There was room for the two men to stay in the lambing-room next to the kitchen.

5   Later, as the sun went down behind the hills, the couple and their guests sat in the hut eating tender pieces of pink-fleshed trout finely grilled over charcoal embers. There were also noodles, peppers and young bamboo shoots, all fried and served with the

fish the girl had caught. The old shepherd, Wei Shan, had led them to find wild garlic, chestnuts, mushrooms and lemon grass to add extra flavours to the meal. He laughed when Jade Fish told him how she had caught her trout.

"I don't catch many trout that way these days," he sighed. "I'm too slow now."

"We never knew where you came from," began his wife as she brought the steaming clay pot to where they were sitting. They looked out at the sheep and the black water buffalo who were grazing peacefully nearby on the mountain grass. "We just found you, or rather, the dog found you, crying on the hillside, an abandoned little baby. So small you were! We fed you on sheep's milk, just like one of our little lambs."

"We called you Jade Fish," said her husband, "because you were wearing that pretty jade necklace that you still have, I see. Yu Yù, we called you. We asked people everywhere but nobody knew who you were or why you had been left out on the hillside. Everyone here was most shocked by the story."

"Perhaps the baby had broken somebody's priceless vase," suggested a deep voice, rumbling with hidden laughter.

Jade Fish looked up startled, but she giggled when she saw that the strange old giant was just teasing her.

"We never wished to give you up," said Wei Shu, the old shepherd's wife with tears in her eyes, "but together we decided that you had the chance of a better life in the town in a big household. The day we left you at the Magistrate's palace I felt my heart breaking."

6   "What happened to Pao Shen, your dog?" Jade Fish asked Wei Shu, while she gently the elderly woman's hand. "How do you round up the sheep?"

"He's become old like us," he answered. "He now lives with another younger couple and is teaching their dog how to look after the sheep. We have few sheep now and they are easily rounded up."

"Could you tell us where and how you found the girl?" suggested Yin Hsi the Gatekeeper. "We're trying to find out her history and where she might have come from."

"Our dog Pao Shen found the baby up by the Steep Rocks Gorge," said the old lady, running her fingers gently through Jade Fish's soft black hair. " He was bringing the sheep down off the mountains for the winter. The little girl was wrapped in a silk shawl."

"Do you still have the shawl?" asked Lao Tzu.

"Of course we do," she answered. "Wei Shan hid it because it was so beautiful and costly. But we could never have sold it, you know."

The old shepherd Wei Shan now rose and went to a wooden trunk at the back of the room. He took out a bundle and opened it up. It was a large drape of deep red silk. Brilliant green dragons were embroidered on it prowling about a silver moon that glowed in the centre. Black silk tassels made a thick fringe all round the sides. There was a silence as they gazed at the beautiful craftsmanship.

"This can only have come from a royal palace," murmured

Lao Tzu. "And it's not from the Imperial Courts in the east, at any rate, for I know their designs. Who is now the monarch of this Zhou region, Yin Hsi? Which warlord exerts power round here and might have left a baby out on the hillside?"

"Ever since the Imperial Court removed to the east and settled in the capital, Chéng-zhōu," answered the Gatekeeper, "it has been the queen, Zhou Ting, who rules in the Palaces of the Peacock Throne. They are thirty leagues distant, or ninety miles away. She became queen because she belonged to the Zhou Dynasty. She married a warlord who is now the regent. He took her name and is known as Zhou Hin but he has never had any real power. It was Zhou Ting, the ruthless queen, who has become the strongest authority in this land.

"Zhou Ting is now ill, we believe, but she and her husband, Zhou Hin still rule with iron fists and nobody dares to stand against them. They're wealthy and very powerful warlords. I should know, for I'm part of the army which keeps them in place. Here they aren't answerable to the Imperial Court of Chéng-zhōu. Anybody who even thinks of trying to resist their power risks instant imprisonment and even execution."

"Ah, yes, all these foolish power struggles!" sighed Lao Tzu. "How many rulers have I seen rise and fall in my time? To lead people you should be like these people here, these good shepherds. All that is needed is to walk behind the people, just as a shepherd does with his flocks, protecting their rear yet able to see dangers ahead. The very best leaders don't put themselves ahead of the people. Too many rulers make that mistake."

"Sir," said the shepherd. "You aren't a king yourself, are you? You sound as if you know a lot about them."

"I know of only bad kings, I'm afraid," muttered Lao Tzu, chuckling to himself. "The wicked leader is the one whom the people all despise. The good leader is the one whom the people all revere. But do you know who the truly great leader is?"

They all shook their heads.

"The great leader," said the Master, smiling, "is the one where the people say afterwards, '*We did it by ourselves!*'"

7 The next morning, after exercising in the sunshine amongst the grazing sheep, Lao Tzu spoke to the elderly couple.

"For your safety, my good friends, I should keep that precious shawl hidden. We shall try to discover more about whether these Zhou monarchs might have left this girl to die as a baby out on the bare mountain, and for what reason. Thank you for your hospitality."

"Thank you, Wei Shu and Wei Shan," said Jade Fish. "I have nothing but good memories of my childhood with you. I shall return here again one day to see you now that I know where you are, so I don't want to say goodbye to you."

At that moment a shaggy brown dog with floppy ears came bounding up the road and he rushed into the girl's arms. It was Pao Shen. He definitely did want to say goodbye. He was very noisy and his greeting lasted several minutes for he wanted to greet everybody and especially Shuïniù, who excited his curiosity because he'd never seen a water buffalo before in these hills. His new master had sent him up to see what was going on. Many others in the huts nearby must also have been wondering, for it was odd how groups of local villagers could be seen sitting or standing outside their homes, gazing upwards at the hut of the elderly shepherd couple.

The travellers set off once more on their journey with some food, lovingly packed by Wei Shu, the shepherd wife. Besides rice there were fresh herbs, beans, pieces of squash and slices of dried duck. There was also ginger preserved in sugar and a pot of honey. Everything was packed carefully into the bags on the buffalo's back. Pao Shen, the dog, who knew the mountains better than anybody else, was finally allowed to lead them up to the Steep Rocks Gorge and the mountain pass that led on towards the Zhou Palaces of the Peacock Throne.

"Send him back when you reach the top of the pass," said Wei Shan, the Shepherd. "He's very obedient."

8   To reach the royal palaces of Zhou Ting you had a six-day journey to cross the Snow Peak Mountains in order to reach the Five Grasses Plains and the wide valleys of Northern Zhou. These plentiful lands were where the farmers grew sorghum, millet, soya, rice and wheat, in such quantities that over the years the kingdom of Zhou Ting had become extremely wealthy.

Lao Tzu was curious about the ruler, Zhou Ting, a queen

with so much power, apparently. With all the wealth from such prosperous farming, Yin Hsi told them as they walked up the mountain track, there came great power, which increased when the mightier Zhou kings of the south-west had moved the Imperial Court to Chéng-zhōu in the east. Zhou Ting's wealth, he said, had built the Western Walls, and she forbade all commerce and all contact across the frontier. Merchants of the west, however, in the Forbidden Lands of the Qin, were allowed in to trade over the border on a daily basis, but only if the commerce was deemed profitable for the Zhou traders. Zhou Ting's power ensured at least that people could live and work in peace, though they had little freedom and no possibility of deciding their lives.

There was much less crime in the towns, continued Yin Hsi, the Gatekeeper and Guard of the Border Town, but the people didn't like their Zhou rulers. These two warlords were cold and ruthless, keeping to their palaces and hoarding their wealth. They dealt very strictly with anybody disobeying the rules, and there were so many of these: water regulations, land regulations, subsoil rights, topsoil rights, lending rules, borrowing rules, codes for conduct and harsh penalties for misconduct.

Lao Tzu sighed a big sigh and clucked his tongue.

"They have been learning all of that from the Qin in the west. It is the Qin who deliberately keep their people oppressed with very strict rules and regulations."

They stopped near the top of the pass to watch the rushing, white waters that bounced and flailed their way down the Steep Rocks Gorge in the direction of the shepherds' village.

The sun was hot but the breeze was cold. It was here that little Jade Fish, wrapped in a plush, red silk shawl emblazoned with green dragons, had so luckily been found by Pao Shen. The dog seemed to remember the occasion and he led them to the exact spot with his tail wagging joyfully and his red tongue hanging out in delight at his cleverness. Jade Fish knelt beside the dog and kissed him lovingly, her arms around his woolly neck.

Then the girl stood up and pointed down the steep, rutted track beside the thunder-filled gorge.

"Go back home, Pao Shen!" she commanded sharply, her voice echoing strangely from the opposite side of the high ravine.

"You can't come with us and you are needed at home for the sheep. Go home!"

The dog was sad and whined, looking up at the girl's face for a change of heart. But she repeated her strict words and Pao Shen, with his tail between his legs as if he had just been banished and sent into exile as a punishment, slunk off obediently and trotted back down the mountain path. He turned and barked hopefully, just once, but the girl didn't call for him to come back.

He knew his way without further telling and he was soon lost to their view.

"You can harden your heart, Jade Fish," said the old man gently. It was almost a question.

"I can," stated the girl sorrowfully. "I have to sometimes. I know what has to be done."

9   The pass continued to wind its way a little further beside the rushing stream between even steeper gorges. Mountains loomed mistily above their heads and all was dark and dank. Finally, they reached the top of the pass, and at that moment the clouds miraculously cleared and they had a magnificent view down into the deep valleys on the other side. There were high mountains still on both sides of the road, but from their vantage point the travellers gazed down at fluffy clouds far below them. These were floating gently over a series of lower foothills leading to a sun-filled plain beyond. There, a broad river snaked its glossy way in the far distance through a patchwork of fields and wide meadows for as far as the eye could see.

Over the horizon and too remote to be seen yet, Yin Hsi told them, there was a walled town with several large palaces surrounded by gardens. These belonged to the Zhou warlords,

"Those would be the ornate Peacock Palaces of Zhou Ting and her husband," said the Master, shielding his eyes with both hands from the afternoon sun, which beamed down strongly on his large weather-beaten head. "I've never been there, though I've read about the Court of the Peacock Throne. I once met the queen's First Counsellor, her eminent ambassador, the Emissary, Bien Manchu. We shall not see the palaces properly for several days yet."

"From up here all that country seems blessed with so much beauty," remarked the Gatekeeper. "It is strange to think that the Zhou Palaces of the Peacock Throne should have acquired such an infamous reputation. How can palaces like those bestow such power?"

"Always remember that what makes a building is not the walls themselves, but the spaces between the walls," said the Master gently. His deep voice sounded like the wind at night, powerfully but safely gusting through majestic trees.

"People are too concerned with materials like stone, wood, clay and iron. Yet it's the emptiness that these materials enclose which is far more interesting. We should think more highly of emptiness. If you're empty you have little to lose and so much to gain.

"And right now, particularly," he continued, "we should be thinking of the emptiness of our stomachs. Yu Yù, our Jade Fish, what do you suggest we do?"

"There's a cave over there, Master, by that stream," the girl replied, pointing to a dark opening at the base of the cliff, in the shadow of whose precipitous ledges they were standing. "We could camp there for the night and light a fire. I could cook you a marvellous feast with what Wei Shu packed for us. After all, that is my training as a Kitchen Girl."

"The person who knows that enough is enough will always have enough," said Lao Tzu in his cryptic fashion.

"You're right, Master," remarked Yin Hsi, " and here we have even more than enough. There's water, food, shelter and good companionship."

"You forgot fuel, Yin Hsi!" said Lao Tzu, smiling. "But look! There's even wood in abundance further down the trail. Why don't you and I go to search for firewood with Shuïniù the Water Buffalo and we'll leave Jade Fish to prepare our supper?"

The bags were unpacked, the bedrolls laid out on the stone floor of the cave, which was clean and smooth. Then the Master and the Gatekeeper left with the Water Buffalo to search for good dry sticks from the pine trees below.

Give way and you will overcome;
Bend yourself to become straight;
Empty yourself and you will find fullness;
Wear things out if you wish to find them new;
Have little and you may gain;
Have much and you will only find confusion.

(**Tao Tê Ching** - The Classic of the Way and Its Virtue - XXII)

PART THREE

If I have even the merest shred of good sense,
Then once I have set off on my Way, I shall not stray from my Path.
The road is not hard to follow,
Though people are tempted to try new tracks...
Some wear gorgeous clothes,
Carry sharp swords, glut themselves
And have more possessions than they can use.
These are robber barons,
And they do not follow the Way of Tao.

(**Tao Tê Ching** - The Classic of the Way and Its Virtue - LIII)

I   As the sun retired below the western horizon, Jade Fish finished preparing the food and was waiting for Lao Tzu and Yin Hsi to return with a third and final load of wood.

Suddenly a horse galloped up the road leading towards the plains far below and a fierce-looking warrior leapt down from his high saddle. He had a brown leather helmet, a grey fur jerkin and black leather leggings. Great boots of grey fur came to just below his knees. Drawing a long, curved sword, he strode towards the cave. He was tall, well-built and his eyes glittered dangerously.

"Who are you, child?" he shouted sternly at the girl. "This is my cave! Who's here with you?"

"I'm alone, sir, as you can see," answered Jade Fish nervously, thinking to reveal as little as possible. "I didn't know this was your cave."

"I own everything here!" snapped the man. Close to, she could see he had a very tanned, smooth-featured face, with long black hair tied at the back and short black moustaches. Particularly impressive were his eyebrows, which were dark and bushy above his sharp, angry eyes. "I'm the lord of this pass, amongst many others, and all who come this way must pay me tribute. It's usually everything they have that is of any worth."

His eyes scanned the floor of the cave.

"Three bedrolls! Saddlebags! So you, girl, are not alone."

He wrenched open the saddlebags and drew out several scrolls. Each was a roll made of thin slivers of bamboo stitched together. He threw them down on the floor in disgust when he saw they were blank and unused.

"Your parents must be nearby," he shouted at the girl, his voice echoing around the cave. "I hope they have their jewels and treasure with them, for there's little else here I can see of any value."

"We're poor travellers," said Jade Fish. "But we have rich food. Won't you eat with us, sir?"

"Eat? Eat with you?" growled the man. "You'll be lucky if you escape with your lives! What's that around your neck?"

He reached forward and grabbed at the pale emerald jade fish. The girl put up no resistance, but stared up at him with a fierce expression in her green eyes that matched his own.

"That's mine!" she replied sharply. "It's all I have of any worth, but you'll have to kill me before I let you have it!"

She then bit hard into one of the strong fingers holding the green fish.

The man jerked his hand back in pain. He opened his own mouth wide showing white, razor-sharp teeth, but then he laughed and sucked his fingers ruefully.

"I admire your spirit, girl! We'll see whether I have that necklace or not. I could wrench it off your neck!"

A deep but gentle rumbling of laughter sounded from behind him. It resembled far-off thunder rolling around bare hilltops before some tremendous storm.

"I would suggest, my good sir, that you refrain from doing that!" said a mild voice. It sounded like gravelly rocks avalanching to some stony valley-floor from a great height.

The warrior spun round and crouched in the firelight, picking up and whirling his large sword with both hands.

"Two old men!" he snarled. "Ha! I shall make mincemeat of both of you, even you, the tall one with the helmet. You, I see, are a Zhou Border Guard. Little good will it do you! Throw down your wealth right now or else I'll hack you both into small pieces!"

2   At a sign from Lao Tzu, both men started stacking their wood against the cave wall. Then they went and sat down near the fire. They took absolutely no notice of their new and unbidden guest.

"Won't you serve us some of that delicious food, Jade Fish?" asked the ancient giant with the enormous ears and a broad belly. "Perhaps this gentleman here will have some with us? He looks hungry enough and the hour is getting late."

"Stop!" shouted the armed newcomer furiously. "I told you to throw down your wealth. Elderly travellers *always* carry plenty of wealth."

"So we do, my friend!" laughed Lao Tzu, holding up a bowl for Jade Fish to serve him from her cooking pot. "Only, all my wealth is up here in my head. In order to have it for yourself, my dear sir, you'd have to take this" – pointing at his head – "from these" – pointing at his shoulders. "But then the head would be virtually useless and any wealth there would surely go to waste."

His shoulders shook as he roared with laughter.

"You're making fun of me?" hissed the man more angrily than ever. His dark eyes bulged, as he looked from one to another. In his fury he strode up and down, swinging his flashing sword as he spoke.

"You! The one dressed as a Border Guard. You'll die first unless you hand over your riches. My sword will sever your scrawny neck, just as I'd lop off the head of an old hen."

"Aren't you Yuan Song, the Robber Baron?" asked Yin Hsi imperturbably, also holding up his bowl to be served by Jade Fish. "If you are, you're wanted by the authorities for murder and robbery. They speak of you in my town on the Border."

"Ha! So they talk of my exploits in the Border Town, do they? Do they mention my prowess with the sword?"

"No," answered Yin His placidly. "They say you're greedy for gold and you're ready to rob and kill innocent travellers to gain it. They say nobody likes or respects you apart from your gang of robbers. It's said, in the Border Town, where I'm the Gatekeeper, that everyone detests your arrogance. They condemn your flouting of the rule of law and the codes of common decency. What can you spend your gold on, anyway? Do you think you'll really find happiness that way?"

"Come, sir," said Lao Tzu with a wide smile creasing his huge face. "Yin Hsi is giving you a remarkably hard time of it. I'm sure you're probably not nearly as bad as he makes out. Sit down with us, and Jade Fish will give you some of her delicious duck broth. You must be hungry after a tiring day in the saddle. All this anger and noise isn't good for anybody."

He held out a fourth bowl for the girl to ladle soup into. But Yuan Song, the Robber Baron, was still far too angry to listen properly. He now seized a red woollen thread from the fringe of the blanket on which they were seated. Eyes bulging with fury, he held up the long thread with his left hand.

"You can't win me over with your clever words, my fine masters!" shouted Yuan Song. "I'm interested in deeds, not words. Watch this!"

The Robber threw the thread up into the air. It floated upwards in the firelight. Then he gripped the great sword with both hands and twirled it so quickly that it became a blur in the glow of the dancing flames. First it whipped one way, with a deep swish, and the thread became two equal pieces while it was still rising. Then it flashed back a second, and then a third time. The two strands of red wool became three strands and then four, of almost equal lengths.

As the four strands of wool floated down to lie on the sandy floor of the cave, Yuan Song's sword was already snapping back into its jewelled sheath at his belted waist. The man crossed his arms, a stern look on his handsome face as he waited for a response from his captive audience.

"Bravo, my dear sir!" said Lao Tzu clapping his hands together enthusiastically. "There can't be many men alive who could do such a thing with a sword. Just as there can't be many girls dishing up pieces of duck in such a tantalising vegetable broth as this, right now."

He took the steaming bowl back from Jade Fish and held it up to the Robber.

"It would be a shame to eat standing up," said the Master, smiling behind his abundant white whiskers. "Will you not sit down with us and rest your weary legs? All this extraordinary sword work must make you hungry by nightfall. Here's your soup, sir!"

There was a long pause while Lao Tzu stared deep into the Robber Baron's eyes.

The man couldn't hold his gaze and dropped his eyes. Strangely, it looked as if there were tears in them. Were they tears of frustration, or could they have been tears of recognition?

Reluctantly, it seemed, and as if he were in a dream where

everything has slowed down, the Robber took his bowl from the Master. He even muttered something that might have been thanks. Then he sat down, but before he could eat he had furtively to wipe a few more tears from his eyes with his sleeve.

3   At the start there was an appreciative silence while they all drank the good soup and formed balls of rice with their fingers to go with the pieces of steaming duck and spicy vegetables.

"You are indeed a good cook," admitted the Robber to the girl whom he had been threatening to behead only a few minutes before this. "Where are you all travelling?"

Lao Tzu briefly explained that they were trying to help the girl to find her parents or guardians from the past. The Robber looked more closely at the sculptured pendant of the jade fish around the girl's neck.

"That's a fine piece of jewellery," he admitted reflectively. "It's well carved and I imagine it must be worth a great deal."

"A man like you, sir," said Lao Tzu, "will doubtless have many fine cooks and much knowledge of such jewellery. Where's your home, if I might inquire?"

"Do you think to trap me?" growled the Robber defensively. "There's a price for my head."

"Ah, so *your* head, too, is worth a fortune? That might be interesting information!" chuckled the Master. "However, we're not interested in wealth."

"How so? Not interested in gold?" asked Yuan Song, the Robber Baron. "Everyone, surely, is interested in acquiring riches?"

"How much happiness, then, has gold and robbery ever brought you?" asked Yin Hsi. "Have you a wife and children to care for and who care for you in return? Here, have some more broth, sir, with your rice?"

There was a long silence and they all waited for the Robber Baron to answer. Strangely, all that he seemed able to do was to stare at Lao Tzu, his soup neglected on the ground before him. The Master paid him no attention for he was clearly more interested in wiping out the bottom of his bowl with a piece of flat bread.

"I will tell you the truth," muttered Yuan Song. "I've never told anybody this before and I'm only telling you because you shared your meal with me. In reality, you are right, gold has never brought me much relief for my loneliness. It's true that people seem to despise me as well as fear me. I once had a wife and a child but they are here no more. How could you have a family life if you're a famous outlaw?"

"A man can always change," suggested Lao Tzu, looking up once more and meeting at last the Robber Baron's earnest eyes. "Embracing change and learning the Way of emptiness and non-striving takes more courage perhaps than twirling a sword, but such a journey is the only guarantee of true happiness. We are all three of us on just such a journey."

"Where are you going, then?" asked the Robber Baron curiously.

"A good traveller has no fixed plans and is not intent on arriving," stated Lao Tzu, beaming. He laughed out loud at Yuan Song's evident confusion.

"That makes no sense!" said the Robber and he looked down at his empty plate. "When you speak, sir, I... I'm suddenly not sure of anything I knew before."

"Not being sure of anything is an excellent start," said Lao Tzu happily. "Yuan Song, do you have the patience to wait until your mud settles and the water is clear?"

"I don't know... sir..., but I think that I might like to change my life. Maybe I could help you. Perhaps I could even travel with you? You would have my protection."

"Then tell me truly, Yuan Song," questioned the huge old man, now leaning forward and staring deeply into the man's eyes, "how many people have you murdered for this yellow metal that you craved so much? How many lives have you hurt and upset?"

"I... I have murdered very few, sir," replied the Robber Baron, dropping his eyes, perhaps in shame. "Most people give me what I ask for out of fear. You are the first people I've met who seem to have no fear."

"Only from caring comes real courage," asserted Lao Tzu. "Those who conquer others may be strong, but those who conquer *themselves*, these are the truly mighty ones."

"I murdered a monk once," confessed Yuan Song. "He refused to part with his gold. I killed two soldiers, accidentally, when they were chasing me across a ravine many years ago."

"Then you will have to find their families later and try to

make amends for what you once did," said Lao Tzu. "That will be very hard for you when the time comes, but you shall not find contentment in this life until you've done this and paid for other mistakes you've made."

"Should I make sacrifices to gods and seek riches in heaven, then?" asked the man humbly, unbuckling his belt and laying down his sword.

"I don't concern myself with gods and spirits, either good or evil, nor do I serve any," replied Lao Tzu. " Serving phantoms and making up more rules and rituals isn't the true way of the Tao. But I can tell you this now, Yuan Song. Listen to me carefully! Unless you change the direction of your life you *may* end up travelling along the road that you are now heading down!"

Then he roared again with laughter, a great gust of it, which filled the cave and frightened the poor Water Buffalo, who was quietly grazing just outside. She gave a great "Moo-errr!" of bovine disapproval.

"I'm afraid the Master often speaks in such riddles," said Yin Hsi apologetically.

"In truth, I should like to learn more from this man," said Yuan Song, scratching his head in puzzlement. "Might I accompany you on your travels... if you please?"

"Why did you come here, this evening?" asked Lao Tzu curiously, still chuckling. "This is a strange place to come on your own. Where are all your faithful followers?"

"I don't know," said the Robber Bandit who was going to be a robber no more. "I come here often just to get away from people.

My followers are on occasion tiresome and demanding. I... I... sometimes feel that I've nothing of any worth to give, either to them or to myself. Much around me has become hollow."

"Hollowness has much virtue," nodded Lao Tzu, smiling. "So has humility. Think of the wide ocean. See how big and majestic it appears. The ocean is vast and it seems to rule the world. And yet, all the rivers run towards it. Why? Because it's set lower than them. Put yourself below other people and you will become the greater for it."

There was a pause while his listeners digested this last piece of wisdom.

Yin Hsi rubbed his nose reflectively and went to make sure that Shuïniù the Water Buffalo was comfortable for the night. Yuan Song took the dishes with Jade Fish to wash them in the river. He carried a blazing brand from the fire to light their way. Lao Tzu sat chuckling to himself and tugging at one of his great ears. Then he built up the fire for the night and unrolled his bedding.

For it was time to sleep.

4   They were woken in the morning by the snorting and whinnying of another horse outside. Yuan Song was shouting at someone in another of his terrible rages. The person was shouting back loudly and afterwards could be heard galloping off, the thudding of hooves resounding above the rushing waters from the mountain torrent nearby.

"What was all that noise about?" asked Yin Hsi mildly when

the Robber Baron came striding back crossly.

"He was a messenger sent by my followers," said Yuan Song still fuming with anger. "The band of thieves I lead are worried that I didn't come back. I know they will certainly not approve of my decision. The messenger said I should expect a knife between my ribs from now on."

"Aha! What it is to be loved and missed by your friends!" joked Lao Tzu. "Perhaps sticking a knife in your ribs would show how much they really *cared* for you!"

To the surprise of everyone, Yuan Song suddenly lay down on the ground and started roaring with laughter. Tears streamed from his eyes and his muscular shoulders shook with amusement. Gasping, he finally sat up, still laughing.

"I'm not used to jokes, sir! You've no idea how funny that was! I suddenly feel so free this morning. I know I shouldn't have lost my temper with the messenger for he was only doing his job. My anger is something I will have to work on, I think. I'll go later and meet with my poor followers. Perhaps they will begin to see life differently when they hear what I have to tell them. Either that or else, perhaps, I *might* yet receive a dagger between my ribs. But whatever happens from now on, I'll have no need of this any more."

He took up his beloved sword in its jewelled, silver scabbard and with no more ado he strode to the river. Standing on the stony bank of the fast flowing stream he drew the shining blade from its sheath, kissed it once and then threw it far into the middle of the swirling torrent of white water. He hurled the elaborate scabbard to join it. Then he laughed again.

"Jade Fish," said Yuan Song, the Robber, a little later, "there's a Wise Woman, who lives alone up in the hills, a few hours' walk from here. Most people think she's mad, for she is wild and half-crazy, but many people nevertheless visit her for advice. She may be able to help you in your search. She knows the Book of Changes and can read the yarrow stalks."

"The *I Ching*? Ah, now, she sounds like a woman after my own heart," cried Lao Tzu, beaming with sly amusement. "What was her advice to *you*, my friend, for it sounds as if you've consulted her already, perhaps?"

"Yes, Master. She said... The woman said that I was too stupid to make a good robber," confessed the Robber Baron, hanging his head with shame at the memory. "At the time I was so angry I cut all the ropes of her shelter and I left her struggling and floundering under the canvas. Now I can see that... she *may* have been right. She's certainly a strange woman, for she seems to know everything."

"Knows *everything*? Ah, then she really is a woman after my own heart!" exclaimed Lao Tzu. "I mustn't set eyes on her or else I'll wish to marry her on the spot, and I'm far too old to marry again. So, you will all kindly leave me here to start working on my scrolls. Come back soon and tell me what this sage woman says."

"Ah, Master," confided Yin Hsi, "I'm so glad you said you wish to set down your teachings! I was afraid you might never get started with your work."

"It shouldn't take too long, Yin Hsi," replied the Master

serenely. "There are eighty-one chapters but most are very short. Indeed, eighty-one chapters is eighty-one too many already, but I suppose that can't altogether be helped."

"Master," demanded the former Robber Baron eagerly, "what should I tell my brother thieves when I see them? Haven't you some simple rules of life?"

"All the best rules of life *are* simple, Yuan Song," declared Lao Tzu. "But here is what you can tell your followers straight away. If they stick to these precepts there is a fair chance that both they and you will lead happier lives and contribute more to this world of marvels."

"What are these instructions, I beg you?" asked Yuan Song, putting his smooth brown face up close to Lao Tzu's so that he wouldn't miss a word.

"In dwelling," answered the Master, "live close to the ground. In thinking, keep to the simple. In conflict, be fair and be generous. In governing, don't try to control. In work, do what you enjoy. In family life, be completely present. There, that's plenty of good advice to start you off!"

"Simple enough," admitted Yuan Song, "but it sounds as if I should try to find myself a family.".

"You could do worse," laughed Lao Tzu. "Being deeply loved by someone gives one strength, while loving someone deeply, as I said before, gives one real courage."

"Come, let's go and find this Wise Woman," suggested the Gatekeeper, who was keen to return to his own dear wife and who didn't want to leave the shutting of the town gates to others for too long.

The Master stood outside the cave waving them farewell. Shuïniù the Water Buffalo would stay to keep him company.

5   The weather suddenly changed, as it so often does up in the mountains. A chill wind now whistled through the pass bringing with it flurries of icy snow and occasional bursts of hail. Yuan Song went and pulled a thick, furry blanket from one of his saddlebags to put around Jade Fish, who was beginning to shiver in her thin cotton clothes and simple woollen shawl. She sat up on his fine horse while the two men walked. The wind howled between the rocks as if it were a creature in pain.

"How did you become acquainted with the Master?" Jade Fish asked the Gatekeeper. She was now wrapped up warmly and wearing some thickly knitted socks and a knitted bonnet which Yuan Song carried with him.

"He found me many months back," replied Yin Hsi. "I received messages and letters from him. He knew I was the Gatekeeper and he wanted to pass to the west, which, as you know is forbidden. He didn't want to cause trouble for me so the messages were sent secretly by people he knew he could trust."

"Do you have children?" the Robber Baron asked the Gatekeeper.

The Gatekeeper told them proudly of his daughter, who was married in the east and expecting a baby soon. They had a son once, he said, but a fatal accident occurred when he was about

Jade Fish's age. The girl looked troubled at this.

"How did he die?" she asked.

"He drowned, swimming in the border river one day," said Yin His quietly. "Although he could hardly swim he dived in to save a friend in difficulties. He saved his friend but then he was swept away by strong currents."

"I'm so sorry to hear that," said Yuan Song. "I, too, had a wife and daughter. She would have been about Jade Fish's age now, but the mother was a poor woman from the hills in the north. One day, she disappeared leaving me no message and taking our daughter with her. I searched and searched the hills to the north, east, and south, but I could find no trace of them."

"That's another sad story," murmured Jade Fish, snuggled up in the blanket. There was just her face peeping out with her eyes continually blinking away the light dusting of snow. "But why did you become a robber, Yuan Song?"

"I had no parents to guide me," he replied. "They died when I was small. I was put into a monastery and monks brought me up. This was in the north of the province. The monks were cruel and unkind and they used the children as slaves. I ran away when I was about Jade Fish's age and fell in with a gang of thieves. These men were cruel and greedy but at least they looked after their own people in a fairer and less selfish way than the monks. Because I was strong and clever with a sword, I eventually became the chieftain."

He sighed.

"I cannot say I am proud of my past. I wish now I could go

back in time and start again. Meeting your Master yesterday has made me reflect about my life."

"Everything about Lao Tzu is extraordinary," assented Yin Hsi nodding, "but he is not *my* Master. He belongs to nobody, and yet to *everybody* at the same time. Wherever he goes, it seems, his strange sayings change people's lives forever. He could have been rich and powerful, working as the Chief Librarian for the Zhou Emperor in Chéng-zhōu in the Yellow River Valley.

"Nobody knows much about him or where he acquired his wisdom. Some say he is two hundred years old. Some say he can fly or that he can do miracles. None of that, I think, is true. But what he says, though it always seems to be dressed up in paradoxes, is immensely practical. Truth rings out of his words like a clear bronze bell. That is what I heard them say in the taverns in the Border Town. He has travelled everywhere and so many people know him, or have heard of him."

"What is that, a... a paradox?" asked Jade Fish hesitantly.

"It is something which sounds contradictory and illogical," answered the Gatekeeper. "For example, if you say, 'I am a liar', that's a paradox, for if you're telling the truth, when you say that, then logically you cannot be telling the truth, but if, on the other hand, you're lying when you say that, then you would be telling the truth, which would totally contradict what you were saying."

"That makes my head spin!" groaned Yuan Song banging his forehead with his fist.

"So, when our Master, Lao Tzu, tells you 'Stop searching, if you want to find', " continued the Gatekeeper, "he wants to make our heads spin, as you call it. Our lives need to change just as our thinking needs to change. The world might become a better place if we listened more and spoke less."

As you might imagine, there was silence for quite a long time after that remark.

6   Back in the cave, Lao Tzu took, from out of a jute sack, rolls of thin flat strips of bamboo that were threaded together on silk rolls. He had made them himself, so he knew that there were eighty-one strips made up in several rolls. He took his brush and a stone inkwell and collected water from the stream. As it was cold he also lit a fire and made himself a pot of tea. If you wish to enjoy your work, he repeated to himself, then you should make yourself thoroughly comfortable.

Laying out the first strip of bamboo vertically on the ground he dipped his brush in the ink and began to trace the small characters easily, with only one noticeable hesitation. There was a smile on his great lips as he worked, for his Tao Tê Ching began with a paradox straight away.

'   *The Tao (or Way) that can be spoken of is not the true Tao.'*

Now, why write any more, if the Way cannot be spoken about?

The Master stared at what he had just written and pondered. Shouldn't he just throw away his scrolls? Was written teaching meaningless and pointless, after all? He laughed.

"He who obtains has little; he who scatters has much," he murmured to himself.

So he went on with his work, but this time he drew the characters with no hesitation.

7   "What is this Book of Changes that you and the Master mentioned?" asked Jade Fish, as the three travellers climbed higher into the bleak heathland of the bare mountains. They were now above the tree-line and the mountainside consisted of rock and brushy scrubland.

"It's called the I *Ching*," answered the Robber Baron. "I know little about it. Just that it is based on a very, very old book used in divination for telling people's fortunes. You have to ask the Book of Changes a question, for it is almost like a person. It is a little like your Master, I think. It answers with riddles. They sometimes seem like nonsense but as often as not they contain truth and wisdom. I had need of many answers when I came here last, but I think I wasn't prepared to listen properly."

"Yuan Song is quite right," agreed Yin Hsi. "The book is like an oracle. You use forty-nine yarrow stalks to find one of the Hexagrams and the Book then tells you about yourself and about how things might change. You see, the Hexagrams are made up of yin and yang lines, which can change according to the numbers and sequences by which the yarrow stalks are drawn.

"When we were married, my wife insisted that we consulted the *I Ching* and we drew the Hexagram called *Chun*. It's all to do with *Difficulty at the Beginning*, which sounds rather unfortunate, especially just at the start of our married life. However, the man who read our fortune explained that it's to do with the chaos that happens with all beginnings, whether of earth or heaven. The Hexagram shows that if you can accept the difficulties, then you can move on and create better conditions. In the end, it corresponded exactly to what happened in our lives and we often think back and talk about the Reading we received from the Book of Changes."

"So shall I have my fortune told?" asked Jade Fish. "Is it certain?"

"Nothing is ever certain," answered Yuan Song, "but if the Wise Woman is there, I'm sure she'll try to see what your future looks like according to the Book of Changes."

Yin Hsi nodded at this and they continued up the steep path.

8　　"If you want your horse back," offered Jade Fish, a little later, "I'm quite used to walking."

"That's all right," replied Yuan Song, the Robber Baron, panting somewhat from the steepness of the rocky track. "It's better that you should ride. We're nearly there. Look! That's her shelter up there."

High above theur track stood three tall pines, the only trees remaining on the mountainside. The tree-line was far below. Here, the lonely pines were even above the clouds, which swirled like puffs of dragon smoke down near the other trees far beneath. The air was cold but the sun was shining at last.

It was early evening and bright rays slanted down from the west lighting up a very powerful waterfall. Rushing water careered down through a deep rift further up the mountain and then tumbled noisily down in a gushing, white stream. The river ran between the group of three pine trees and a strange shelter, which they could see just beyond. They watched as the water dashed over a wide rocky ledge high above their heads and then fell past them into a turbulent pool far below, before racing onwards in fast flowing currents, bouncing and flailing over the black rocks in its path. A glittering rainbow hovered above the thundrous rapids casting its magical colours in a beautiful arc.

"How can we cross such a river?" shouted the Gatekeeper above the roaring of the waterfall. They were pressing on past the tall pine trees, who stood like sentries at attention guarding the Wise Woman's home. There was no sign yet of anybody living there.

"Come, I'll show you," said the Robber Baron.

He led his mare towards the deafening cataract with Jade Fish sitting astride her. The horse began to shy away in fear, but Yuan Song spoke gently to her saying there was nothing to fear, and he drew her on to a dark entrance behind the torrent of falling water. Spray and spume hissed at them and there was a spattering of fine foam at their feet, but after they had entered the black hollow the three travellers discovered a surprise.

Behind the waterfall was a deep cave. It had been carved out no doubt by the passage of water over thousands of years. The floor was sandy and dry but a little further forward, in front of their wondering eyes, hundreds of tons of white-curtained thunder came crashing past them down to the tumultuous pool below. A thick green light passed through this wall of tumbling water, quite different from any other light in the world. It was like green jade, but dancing and sparkling in wild patterns over the cave floor and along the smooth grey walls.

How easy it would have been to stand there for hours entranced by the light and lulled by the roaring of the cascade! They knew, however, that they couldn't wait but must press on to seek out the Wise Woman, if she were still there.

9   The shelter was an extraordinary assemblage of spars of wood, canvas and interwoven branches of brushwood, all plastered over with clay. The branches rested on great rocks and were roofed with slabs of slate. The cold wind had died away and smoke now began to drift skywards, kissing the branches of the great pine trees as it rose. It smelled sweetly of burning pine resin and seasoned mountain oak. Behind the shelter was a great stack of neatly arranged firewood with some large logs ready for splitting.

There was no door barring the way; instead there was a thick, black pelt with a ferocious bear's head still attached at the top. This heavy bearskin curtain hung from an oak lintel and was protected by an overarching porch made of wooden wattles and daubed clay. The bear's black head stared out sightlessly over the world, its great jaws wide open showing huge, dark-stained ivory fangs. It made an impressive and fearsome gatekeeper.

With the noise of the river still ringing in their ears, the travellers stood uncertainly on the threshold, which in this case was one massive paving slab, polished by the elements - the size of a small courtyard. A dog barked from the back of this home.

Suddenly, the bearskin was pushed aside from within and the figure of a woman slowly emerged.

Tao resides in taking no action
Yet nothing is left undone.
If princes and lords followed this principle
Ten thousand things would all develop naturally...

(**Tao Tê Ching** - The Classic of the Way and Its Virtue - XXXVII)

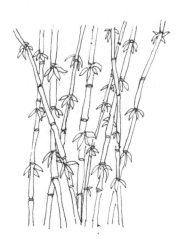

PART FOUR

The ancient masters were subtle, mysterious, and deep
With unfathomable insight. How can it be described?
Let me tell you how they appeared –
Wary, like those crossing a stream in winter,
Watchful for danger.
Courteous like guests paying a visit,
Yielding, like ice ready to melt,
Hollow like caves,
Opaque, like muddied pools.

Who is it, then, who can wait quietly until their mud settles?

(**Tao Tê Ching** - The Classic of the Way and Its Virtue - XV)

I   The Wise Woman was tall but not as tall as Yin Hsi. She had a striking face with almond-shaped eyes set quite far apart above high cheekbones. Her skin was nut-brown and smooth, like softened lambskin. She might have been any age from forty to twice forty years old: it was quite impossible to tell. Her dark hair was tied up behind in a black, woollen headdress and she wore a heavy black woollen cloak.

"I've been expecting your return for some time now, Yuan Song," were her first words. "Your life, I know, is in urgent need of change, but I wasn't expecting your friends or family as well. Please come this way."

She led the way into the main living room. It was dark but warm and it smelled of cedar wood mingled with scents of jasmine and musky rosewater. There were two cats who were asleep in a basket in front of a big log-fire in the rough, stone-lined fireplace.

The Robber Chief looked uneasy but he introduced his new companions and explained that they had come on account of the girl, Jade Fish. For himself, he said, his life had suddenly changed without even the assistance of the Wise Woman.

"How so?" asked the woman sharply. "Don't tell me, Yuan Song, that there are no more travellers left to rob? Don't tell me your gang have all left you at last? Don't tell me you have found yourself another wife?"

She laughed and slapped her knees in merriment.

Yuan Song looked even more embarrassed and explained to her that he had met a strange sage whom he had learned to call Master. His name was Lao Tzu.

The woman started, and then she smiled.

"I've heard of this man and I'm certain I met him once. When I was a young girl I met a pilgrim who had this name. He was a librarian, he said, in the service of an emperor. He talked of the Tao, the Path of Infinite Virtue. But that was many, many years ago."

She greeted Jade Fish and immediately noticed and admired her necklace, regarding it closely.

"I know that hand!" she announced. "That is the work of a man called the Jade Cutter. He used to do work for the Court of the Peacock Throne. His work was much sought after."

She inquired about the girl's history and looked particularly interested in the story of the baby in the rich shawl discovered by the shepherds.

"So, my girl," said the Wise Woman, "you wish to consult the Oracle of Changes, do you? What would you like to ask the *I Ching*?"

"I see no oracle," said Jade Fish staring round the dimly lit room where they were standing. There was little light, but there were patterned, woollen carpets on the floor and rich, silk tapestries hung on the walls. The fire blazing in the wide stone hearth cast a flickering glow that lit up the room.

"Where is this Book of Changes?" inquired the girl.

"I have learned the *I Ching*," replied the strange woman. "It is I who speak for the Oracle, my dear. Do you have a question to put to the Book of Changes, I wonder?"

"Madam," answered Jade Fish. "I have no parents as far as I know and I do not know who I am nor where I am going. But these are not questions I wish to put to the Oracle."

"Quite right, child. Questions about one's family or details about journeys are not the best ones to put to the *I Ching*." The woman looked pleased. "You may call me by my name, Jade Fish.

I am Chan Shui. I come from *Water*, you see, *Shui*. Perhaps that is why I like living near water."

"Thank you, Chan Shui," said the girl. "My question then is, 'How shall I become a worthy person?'"

Not receiving an immediate reply, Jade Fish looked up at the Wise Woman, who was studying her carefully.

"What have you got to give me in exchange for a reading of the Oracle?" asked the woman.

Jade Fish looked worried. She glanced at the Gatekeeper and then at the Robber; they were both staring at her to see what she would say.

"But, I have nothing to give you, madam," she said. "I have no riches and I have barely enough clothes even to keep myself warm."

"You have a beautifully carved treasure around your neck, don't you?" said the woman. "I can accept that as payment."

The girl gasped in horror. "But, madam, this is all I have in the whole world! This necklace stands for me, for my name. I cannot possibly give you that."

"You are wrong," said the woman. "You have far more in the world than just a stone fish, however beautiful. You have friends here, who are helping you. You have a Master to educate you. You have a future waiting ahead of you."

The Wise Woman smiled. Was her smile cruel or was it kind? Perhaps it was both.

There was a very long pause.

The girl took a deep breath and there were shining tears

forming in her eyes. She let them trickle down her cheeks as she said humbly,

"You are quite right, madam, and I am wrong. You may have my necklace as your own. I *do* wish to know more about myself and my future, and that is worth more to me than anything."

So saying, she reached up and undid the silver clasp at the back of her neck. She held out the leather band attached to the delicate, green fish. You could plainly see its gills and its fins. You could see every scale of its smooth, glossy body.

The woman took it, considered it carefully and then laughed.

"That's all right, my child! I don't really want your jade fish, lovely though it is. I wished instead to see whether you were serious in your quest to know your future. I am satisfied that you are. When you are ready, as you were, to give up all that you have, then perhaps you may obtain."

"That sounds very much like one of our Master's sayings," commented Yin Hsi drily.

2   "Before we consult the Oracle," said the Wise Woman, "I should be a poor host if I didn't offer you food and drink. You must be hungry by now after your journey."

The woman went around the room lighting tall, sweet-smelling wax candles. After a while the room was glowing with yellow flames which flickered and illuminated the richly coloured tapestries on the walls.

"That's better," she muttered as if to herself. "I was not

expecting such a party of people as this. We need light to see our way."

The visitors sat on a soft carpet of dark reds and faded blues in the middle of the room, and they talked quietly while the woman fetched them tea and bowls of rice. As if by magic, more bowls with vegetables, stir-fried in tempting sauces, arrived on red-lacquered, wooden trays.

"How long have you lived here, Chan Shui?" asked Yin Hsi the Gatekeeper, as the woman poured tea into little porcelain cups.

"I came here when Zhou Ting was quite young," answered the Wise Woman. " I used to live at court, as Yuan Song knows very well, for that is why he came to see me in the past. I had learned the secrets of divination from my mother, and she from her mother. We had a set of apartments and people even came all the way from the far east to consult with me.

"But Zhou Ting's mother was a powerful woman, a Zhou queen who was jealous of my reputation and influence. She didn't like what the Hexagrams pronounced for her son, the Prince Zhou Han, and for my part in reading the yarrow sticks she expelled me from the court. Tragically for all concerned, the prince died the following winter, something which might have been avoided if he and she had heeded the warnings. It was his sister, Zhou Ting, who then claimed the kingdom after her mother's death only a few years later.

"People still come to have their fortunes told by me, so I do not starve and I prefer to live out my days up here in the mountains, away from the intrigues and the corruption of court and city life."

She smiled wryly at the Robber Baron.

"Yuan Song also prefers life in the mountains, isn't that so?" She laughed.

The Robber Baron looked awkward for a moment, but then he raised his eyes and met her gaze.

"My life will surely change now, Chan Shui," he said simply.

3   The Wise Woman cleared the dishes and then sat before her guests on the carpet, with three wax candles on either side of her. The glow of candlelight in the room lent a magical sweetness and warmth to the room. Then she set a heap of dried yarrow stalks in front of her.

"Fifty," she murmured, "and I take one away, so we are left with forty-nine."

She began dividing the pile into two heaps, placing some stalks between her fingers and then counting off stalks on the left side into fours. She did the same with the pile on the right. It was all most complicated and Jade Fish was intrigued.

"Why do you have to follow such a complicated procedure?" asked the girl.

"Because that is the way the *I Ching* is consulted," answered the woman simply. "It has always been done this way. It may seem strange, but perhaps it makes the readings more subtle and therefore more fully developed."

Finally she placed all the sticks in front of her and studied them carefully for several minutes.

The Wise Woman then announced,

"You have obtained the Hexagram called 'Return' or *Fu, The Turning Point*. I shall draw it for you, so you will understand it better."

Saying this, she picked up a piece of chalk and drew a figure on a slate by her side. At the bottom was a long horizontal line and piled on this were five pairs of divided lines, thus:

"This is the Hexagram *Fu*," she continued. "First I shall tell you of the Judgment. Then I shall describe the Image for you, and then I shall interpret the lines of the Hexagram."

"The Judgment says that this is a Return. You are returning. *'Going out and coming is without error. Friends come without blame. To and fro goes the Way. On the seventh day comes the Return. It furthers one to have somewhere to go.'*"

"Let me try to explain," continued Chan Shui, "by using the words of the Oracle. After a time of decay there comes a turning point. The powerful light that was banished now returns. There is movement but it is not brought about by force. Do you see the upper three lines? They form the Trigram called *K'un*. This is characterised by devotion. This makes the transformation of old into new an easy one. The measures accord with the time. New societies of people sharing the same views are formed, but since all is transparent and in harmony with the time, all selfish and separatist tendencies are excluded and no mistakes are made."

"So I am returning and will meet new people who are in harmony with me?" said the girl wonderingly. "I have no idea where I am returning, but I'm glad it's all so positive. "

"It is up to you to keep it so," replied the woman. "According to the Oracle, all movements are accomplished in six stages. For example, there are six months from the summer solstice to the winter solstice, aren't there? So the number seven signifies movement and change. A new beginning.

"Now let me give you the Image that accompanies the Hexagram.

> *"'Thunder within the Earth.*
> *The Image of the Turning Point.*
> *Thus the Kings of antiquity closed the passes*
> *At the time of the winter solstice.*
> *Merchants and strangers did not go about,*
> *And the Ruler did not travel*
> *Through the provinces.'"*

"It all sounds very beautiful but I don't understand any of it," said Jade Fish.

"Ah," murmured the Wise Woman, "you see, the Hexagram *Fu* is talking about a wintry season of the soul, where all is dormant and waiting for renewal. Thunder symbolises a life force, but in winter this life force, bearing rain and new growth, is locked up in the cold earth. There is a better time coming for you after the Turning Point, when you will blossom like a plant flowering in spring."

"Oh, good!" said the girl. "I need something to look forward to!"

"There is Nine at the beginning – we start at the bottom of the Hexagram, so that is the bottom line, which is full. It reads like this:

"*'Return from a short distance.*
No need for remorse.
Great good fortune.'"

The girl seemed pleased and leaned forward intently.

"It means you may wander from the path a little, in the nature of things, but provided the straying is not excessive, no harm will be done.

"*'Six in the second place means:*
Quiet return. Good Fortune.
Six in the third place means:
Repeated Return. Danger. No Blame.'

"In other words, you should be careful that change should not become an end in itself and be undertaken carelessly. You must be careful to seek the good path always.

"*'Six in the fourth place means:*
Walking in the midst of others
One is walking alone.'

"This means that you will be accompanied, but you will have

the sole responsibility for managing your life."

"I understand," said Jade Fish. "I feel sometimes as if I have always been walking alone."

"Yes," said the Wise Woman, "but, you know, that feeling of loneliness is true for all who think about their lives. You are certainly not alone in having that feeling! Let's look at the next line.

'Six in the fifth place means:
Noble hearted return. No remorse'.

"That seems straightforward," she said. "Now we come to the top line,"

"'Six at the top means:
Missing the Return. Misfortune.
Misfortune from within and without.
If armies are set marching in this way,
One will in the end suffer a great defeat,
Disastrous for the ruler of the country.
For ten years
It will not be possible to attack again.'

"Ah! You have to understand, my child, that this is all to be interpreted symbolically," continued Chan Shui, the Wise Woman. "Blind obstinacy and a refusal to accept the opportunities and the responsibilities that come with change will lead to personal disasters. For a ruler that could mean *national* disasters."

There was a silence.

"Thank you, Chan Shui," said the girl, giggling a little. "It's not very likely, I think, that I shall ever be responsible for a national disaster, but I will think carefully on your words. If you will not accept my jade fish I will find another way to thank you."

"Not everything in life needs repayment," said the woman looking hard at the Robber Baron with a wicked smile in her wide-set, almond eyes. The man dropped his eyes in shame and remorse.

He remembered once cutting the ropes that held up her canvas shelter.

4   "Come," she said. "Since you, Yin Hsi and Yuan Song, are both here, and it is cold outside, and we have nothing better to do, I shall read your fortunes as well."

Yin Hsi went first and asked whether he should continue in his job as Gatekeeper. He drew the Hexagram *Hsü*, which is Waiting.

"*'The superior man eats and drinks,*
Is joyous and of good cheer.'

"You should not worry and seek to shape the future by interfering with things before the time is ripe," said Chan Shui. "You must be calm and bide your time."

"Oh, that's a relief!" replied Yin Hsi. "Does that mean that I will remain as Gatekeeper?"

"Yes, you should remain attentive and watchful, and you will be serene."

"What about me, madam?" said the Robber Baron humbly. "I will listen more carefully than I did the last time I was here."

The woman eyed him carefully, and then for a third time she sorted the yarrow stalks, laying them down finally before her on the rug.

"You have drawn the Hexagram *Ku*," she announced. She smiled. "It is called '*Work on What has been Spoiled or Decayed*'. Ah, Yuan Song, it says you must work on regeneration and regrowth. Where there has been corruption, you must work to correct it, but it will have to be done gently and with sound understanding. It must not be too dramatic.

"When the others have gone to bed, I shall explain in greater detail what your Reading involves. Now, however, you may all unroll your bedding and I shall give you more blankets for when the fire dies down. It becomes cold here at night."

She stood up.

"Come out and see the stars, all of you!" she ordered, smiling. "One of the many wonders in the mountains is that the stars are so much clearer than down below."

Above them, outside in the cold night, the planets were turning, so slowly yet so clearly, as if magnified somehow. The river behind them never stopped its soft thunder. They watched, pleasantly deafened by the noise of the water, whilst a full, yellow moon dragged itself up above the blanched peaks to the north. Wisps of fine mist could be spied hanging near the jagged mountainsides. Jade Fish stood enraptured by the spectacle and later in her bed she wondered for a long time about her Turning Point and what could possibly be meant by her 'Return'.

Then, lulled by the roaring waters, she fell into a deep sleep.

5 Early the next morning, Jade Fish rose and washed in the freezing streams of the pounding waterfall. There was a pool among the rocks where the water was almost still and she could see purple rocks and waving emerald weeds below the surface. A large carp speckled with gold lazily rose to the surface, opening and shutting its mouth as though it wished to speak with her.

Returning, she spotted a young horseman standing at the entrance. He had well-fashioned hide clothing with a furred white cap and big black leather boots. Long black hair hung behind him, tied with a red ribbon and his chin boasted a wispy, black beard. Yuan Song was speaking with him at the entrance of the shelter. The young man was furious, for some reason, and he shouted at the Robber Baron before putting his foot in the stirrup and swinging himself up into the saddle. His horse reared up suddenly and the man cried out and galloped off down the track. She noticed that this time Yuan Song had not become angry.

"Who was that?" asked Jade Fish.

Yuan Song sighed. "He is one of my followers. He's a young man I like very much, Ling Hu. I treat him almost as a son. He's very strong and capable, but he's only just sixteen years old and he has the hot-headedness of youth. Ling Hu said the others want me to return straight away. They are all very upset and angry with me. I told him about how I want to change our lives and live according to the Way of Virtue, the Tao. But right now, Ling Hu is utterly enraged that I haven't returned. He told me that they will certainly kill me if I continue to talk about such things. I think he's just frightened. Change always feels like a threat. They look to me to lead them. I'm sure, however, that I will be able to win them over given time."

He went inside saying that he would make tea.

Chan Shui, dressed in black silk trousers and a black silk tunic, presently joined Jade Fish. She led the girl to a grassy platform beside the river a further down the mountain. The river rushed past them and beyond it they had an unspoiled view of the mountains while the sun rose above the horizon. It was a beautiful morning and mists like patchy wood smoke partly hid the valleys. Steamy vapours rose very slowly up the mountainsides, only to dissolve higher up in the gathering warmth of the rising sun.

Together they performed their exercises, the same exercises which Lao Tzu had shown Jade Fish. The girl liked it when the Fair Lady Works at the Shuttles (it was called *Yu Nu Ch'uan Shu*), or when they Waved Hands like Clouds (or *Yun Shou*). They moved in complete harmony and though the exercises were delicate and soft, the young girl and the old woman were poised and ready at all times to defend or attack. When they performed the Repulse of the Monkeys (or *Tao Nien Hou*), she thought of all the bad things in her life, the sorrows and frustrations, and she gently pushed them away from her as she retreated, step by careful step. They both Shot the Tiger with their Bows in the exercise called *Wan Kung She Hu*, and at the end they stood for a moment peacefully as their breathing went calmly in and out. They stared at the river tumbling so rapidly and at the mountains standing so still. The sun continued to rise, dispelling the chills of night.

Life was a series of naturally harmonious opposites which these exercises re-enacted.

Shortly afterwards, they returned to break their fast along with the others. Yuan Song had made tea for them all.

6 "I'm leaving to return to my poor band of thieves," announced Yuan Song after breakfast was finished. "Thank you for talking with me last night. I have decided to tell them all about my change of heart and I shall try to persuade them to return our stolen goods and make reparation for our misdeeds. They may wish to kill me, or perhaps they will listen. I hope, not just for my sake, that they will listen.

"I also wish to find my wife and child, if I can. They may now be living in the far east, for all I know."

"Learn not to seek too hard and you may have a better chance of finding," advised the Wise Woman.

They all said goodbye to the Robber Baron, who swung himself easily up into the saddle of his grey mare. The horse stamped and whinnied, eager to be off, but before he left Yuan Song said,

"I should like to give you all gifts, but since everything I own was stolen and must be returned, I shall not offer you anything at this time. If we meet again, however, you may expect me to try to repay you. I feel as if I can live again."

They watched him pass behind the waterfall as he started his perilous journey back. He waved to them once on his way back down the mountain.

7   "Come with me," said the Wise Woman to Jade Fish. "You may come too, Yin Hsi. I wish to show you something which I've never shown to anybody before now."

She led them to a curtained alcove at the back of the shelter. Behind the curtain was a child's bed and a carved wooden trunk with birds painted on it. Herons and ducks in red lacquer-work were pictured on a shiny black background. Inside the trunk were silk clothes for a girl.

"Like Yuan Song, I, too, once had a daughter, but she died of a fever when she was just thirteen. These things happen, but they are very hard to bear. I miss her every day. I would like you to have these clothes, Jade Fish. They were made by the palace tailors when I was at court, so many years ago."

They were exceptionally fine clothes, with silk suits and shawls made of the finest wool from northern India. Jade Fish had never seen such garments, even at the Magistrate's palace.

"I'm deeply honoured, Chan Shui," she said, "but I could not wear such beautiful clothes. We have no means of carrying them anyway."

"I think you may one day return here and they are here for you. It would please me to think that my daughter's clothes will be used again. Please try them on."

When Jade Fish slipped on a patterned suit of dark green silk, she was suddenly quite transformed. She bowed to the woman, putting her two hands together, and said,

"Truly, these clothes are wonderful, but I cannot wear them.

I must first know who I am and why my parents abandoned me. I fear that I had a troubled beginning, though perhaps now my fortune will change if I can indeed return to where I began my life."

"You may go," said the woman, "but first I shall wash your old clothes, just as I used to do for my daughter and I shall cook for you the carp stew she so loved. Yin Hsi, I know you are impatient to get home, but please accept my hospitality for one more day. I shall enjoy being a mother once more. It will revive good memories."

"Excuse me," said Jade Fish, "but may I ask you who was your daughter's father?"

"Yes, of course you may. Chan Wu was a valiant soldier whom I loved very much. He fought against the Zhou kings many years back. I was taken prisoner after my husband was killed in a battle. I was brought to the Palaces of the Peacock Throne and was confined in the palace dungeons for over a year. I used to tell the fortunes of the other prisoners and the king came to hear about this from the Dungeon Keeper. His Majesty wished to consult the Oracle and I was summoned to tell the ruler his fortune. Strangely, the king came to depend on me more and more. I used to tell fortunes for the whole court and eventually I was given my own apartments in the palace.

"It was his wife, the queen and mother of Zhou Ting, the present queen, who went against me after I read their fortunes. I could see that their son would have a problem and I said so. The queen, however, could not accept the implications of my reading."

"What was the son's difficulty?" asked Jade Fish.

"Zhou Han, the prince, was a sweet boy, but he was not very strong and he hated horses. His royal father, however, was determined that he should go hunting on horseback with the court. I tried to advise a different course because the Oracle had cautioned against such violent sporting activities which were deemed unfavourable, but the parents refused to listen. He later died as a result of a bad fall from his horse. That was when I was sent away from the court with my child."

"I shall return here one day perhaps and would willingly wear your daughter's clothes with gratitude. Nobody has ever offered me such finery," said Jade Fish.

8　That day was a wash day.

All the clothes were washed and scrubbed in the pure, cold, riverwater. Then they were left to dry on the rocks. The sun beat down all day and they dried quickly. In a sweet-smelling wooden chest, Chan Shui found other, more ordinary silk clothes for her guests to wear while the laundry was being done. The Gatekeeper was good at mending things and he went around the shelter fixing doors that didn't shut properly or else repairing hen coops, gates, fence posts or roof tiles.

"Would you like to hear the Dragon?" asked the Wise Woman after they had eaten lightly at midday. "He lives further up the mountain and it is worth hearing him speak. He is fearsome, but not too dangerous if we are careful."

"I didn't think dragons really existed," said Jade Fish. "I thought they were only in stories, like monsters and giants."

"You're probably right," said Chan Shui, "but this particular Dragon really *does* exist and he really *does* speak. You will see. But we shall not take Gŏu the dog. It will frighten him too much."

In the afternoon, under grey wintry skies, they set off up the mountain. To begin with they followed the river, but they later branched off right and began to climb a steep mountain of bare rock. The rock was burnt black or dark red, and no vegetation grew there at all. All around was a scene of utter devastation with no birds, nor plants, nor any cooling streams.

"This is a volcano," explained the woman as they climbed. "It is still active. Do you see smoke rising from that basin up there?"

She was pointing upwards to an area that was lower than the distant peak. The summit was still a long way up and the highest point was covered by wisps of motionless cloud. Below it, there was a circular crater like an amphitheatre. They could see smoke and vapours rising in the cold air.

"He is called *Huŏ Long* or the Fiery Dragon. You will understand why later."

They continued climbing and after another half hour they could see before them the lip of the great basin. As they approached, they could hear a growling every so often, which intensified as they approached. Great puffs of steamy smoke billowed up at these moments.

"Is it safe to go nearer?" asked Yin Hsi, quite alarmed at what he could see and hear.

"Nothing is ever truly safe," said the Wise Woman, "but I have been here many times and I know the Dragon's moods. Today, he is a little perturbed but he is not angry. One learns to stay away from him when he becomes really cross."

She smiled.

They drew nearer and paused under the raised lip of the enormous bowl. They were still protected by the black wall of lava forming the crater rim, and they could not yet look down to the bottom of the inside of the crater.

"Listen!" said Chan Shui. "The Dragon speaks after every sixty heartbeats."

They counted to sixty as they listened.

Suddenly, there was a deep, growling roar from a long way under the earth. The harsh black rocks they were standing on shook slightly at the reverberations from underneath. Smoke and embers were blasted high into the air as if the mountain had coughed up and belched out some burning dregs from its innermost recesses, and spewing them over the frozen lava of the mountainside.

It was frightening, but the woman motioned to them to climb further, right up to the very edge of the crater's lip so they could see down into the dark abyss.

Smoke continued to billow upwards as the roar subsided.

Peering cautiously over the edge of the circular depression they saw a very strange sight indeed. Through thick clouds of dark ash, they watched as yellow and red mixtures slowly swirled and eddied, sliding their way amongst grey, or even green, counter-currents. These stirred and stewed, sucked and spat, like some deeply coloured and highly poisonous porridge that seethed in a molten, mottled mess, down in the very depths of this diabolical pit.

"Is that not the Gateway to the Kingdom of Dragons? Is it not the Land of Demons and Devils, they who torture the dead?" whispered Yin Hsi, awe-struck. He was profoundly shaken by what he was witnessing.

Chan Shui laughed.

"No, I think not. This is all perfectly natural, my friend! Just as there is cold, green seawater in the oceans, so there is red-hot, molten fire in the earth, deep down. Why it is thus, I cannot say, but we know already how exceedingly powerful are the forces of water, wind and fire. Perhaps, then, *this* was how the world was formed in its infancy.

"I believe, just as Lao Tzu also teaches, that there is a natural balance in our lives, between yin and yang. Between light and dark, cold and hot, fullness and emptiness, inner and outer, youth and age, masculine and feminine. In this balance, nothing stops; all changes and shifts, just as our lives keep changing. But, if we can find and master this balance and adjust to the changes accordingly, then our lives and the lives of all around us will change for the better. This, I think, is the aim of the Book of Changes, the *I Ching*.

"Listen! The Dragon is speaking to us once again. Pay close attention to what he has to say."

For Jade Fish it sounded as if *Huö Long* the Fiery Dragon was telling her that there is life and regular breathing, even in the darkest and most inhospitable conditions. That fire and molten minerals can create cold and beautiful mountains. That inner worlds and outer worlds are sometimes pitched together in seeming antagonism, but that together they make up the conditions of life. That cold mountains high up can have hot depths below. That our lives must take account of this balance and harmony. That there is change from one to the other, but that all changes can be controlled and managed rather than just suffered and endured.

The Dragon continued to speak as they set off to go back home. Its words, thought Jade Fish, did not lack wisdom. The winds began to blow, mercilessly cold, and the grey clouds hurried as if they too wished to get home before they became chilled to the bone.

On their return the Wise Woman lit a roaring fire and found herbs to go with the fat carp she wanted to cook for them that evening. Jade Fish offered to clean it, while Chan Shui chopped vegetables and cooked peppery sauces to go with it. The beautiful carp with its golden scales and open mouth looked just like the one which had stared at Jade Fish in the river pool. Perhaps it was a cousin.

Outside the winds might blow cheerlessly, but inside, amongst the warmth and candlelight, there was feasting and friendship.

9   In the morning, the Wise Woman and Jade Fish did their exercises again, though this time dense clouds swirled about their heads in cold winds that brought spattering rain as they finished. They both hurried back up the mountain to the warmth of the shelter.

"Having you to stay has made me very happy," said Chan Shui, the Wise Woman. "I shall miss you very much. It was like having a daughter once more."

"Do you not get lonely up here, all on your own?" asked Yin Hsi, the Gatekeeper.

"I have my chickens, my garden, my cats and Göu the dog," replied the woman. "The mountains keep me company and the pine trees and the river watch over my home. Yes, I miss the company of people, though I do have visitors. Who know? Circumstances can alter and lives may change. One must *gratefully* change what can be usefully changed, and one must *gracefully* accept what cannot be usefully changed."

They packed their bundles and said farewell to the cats. Göu the dog was plaintively asking to come with them.

"I shall accompany you part of the way," said Chan Shui, "for I have to feed my monkey friends. You haven't yet met them, but they already know all about you, for they have been visiting here, unseen by you, in the evening and the early morning. Now, they are waiting for me at their home in the forest lower down. This time we can take Göu the dog with us."

It was midday when they left, passing behind the waterfall.

Golden patterns once more danced on the cave floor behind the crashing wall of water, for the sun had unexpectedly returned.

Göu the Dog was very happy to be taken on the walk. He knew the way and pranced on ahead of the walkers, who followed him, chatting and gazing in wonder at the mountain scenery. Turning from cold wintry weather, the skies had cleared and the world was bathed in warm sunlight that accentuated the dark blue shadows under the green trees and bushes.

They walked down the stony track until they reached the forest. The monkeys, all one big family, queued up to receive the wild carrots which the Wise Woman grew specially for them. The old male was first in line, then his wives and then the younger males and the babies. Unlike most wild monkeys, this troop behaved with the utmost obedience. They clearly respected and liked the Wise Woman who had names for them all and who treated them strictly but amiably, almost as if they were her family.

Once they each had their carrots, the monkeys retreated to the trees, chattering and screeching wildly. They swung themselves precariously across ravines and steep rocks using branches and hanging lianas. They also enjoyed teasing the dog, trying to pull his tail and then leaping up into the trees before he could snap at them. The tail of poor Göu the Dog dropped between his legs. He barked and whined, looking most unhappy.

"You should search for the Jade Cutter," said Chan Shui, after the monkeys had all been fed and had gone off to play elsewhere. "I heard that he was dismissed many years back. He must be an old man by now, but if he's still alive, he could tell you who ordered your jade fish to be carved originally. He used to live in the eastern foothills before he came to work at the court."

The woman looked in the opposite direction from the sun, which was now beginning to descend towards the distant mountains. The foothills could only just be seen in the far distance, over on their right.

"It is a good day's journey or even more," she said pointing out their route. "Ask on the road. He must be well known."

"We shall do so after we have gone back down to the Pass of the Steep Rocks Gorge," said Yin Hsi the Gatekeeper. "We must return there first to find our Master. He is busy writing the Book of Tao. It will become the collection of Lao Tzu's teachings."

"I should like to read that," the Wise Woman said smiling.

"No doubt you will, one day," responded Yin Hsi, " though I think you already know a lot about the Tao."

"Goodbye, Jade Fish," said the woman. "Remember that you are at the Turning Point and that your Way, the Tao, is something you can learn to control and shape to make good things happen. That is the importance of the *I Ching* or the Book of Changes. Perhaps we will meet again some day. I certainly hope so."

"Thank you so much, dear Chan Shui!" said the girl, bowing courteously to the woman. She picked up her modest bundle once more. "I'm in your debt, and I hope to be able to repay you one day. I should like to wear your daughter's clothes soon before I grow too large for them."

They laughed because she was so slender. Chan Shui turned

to climb the track back home, with Göu the Dog happily wagging his tail once more. Yin Hsi and Jade Fish continued on the path down the mountain towards the Pass of the Steep Rocks Gorge. There would be a three-hour walk before darkness fell.

> *That which fails must first be strong,*
> *That which is cast down must first be raised.*
> *Before receiving, there must be giving.*
> *You should shade your light in order to see better.*
> *Soft and weak defeats hard and strong.*

(Tao Tê Ching - The Classic of the Way and Its Virtue - XXXVI)

PART FIVE

Those who know do not speak.
Those who speak do not know.
Keep your mouth shut.
Train your senses.
Soften your sharpness.
Simplify your problems.
Shade your brightness.
Be at one with the dust of the Earth.
Merge with the merest elements...

(**Tao Tê Ching** - The Classic of the Way and Its Virtue - LVI)

I   Night was falling fast by the time that they arrived at the dim cave. As they approached they could see the light of a big fire near the entrance and six horses were tied up close to Shuïniù, who was peacefully grazing close to where they had left her. The seventh horse, standing tethered on its own, they recognised as Yuan Song's grey mare. Yin Hsi put a warning hand on Jade Fish's arm.

"Be very quiet!" he whispered. "I think they're in big trouble. Let's creep up carefully."

Silently and cautiously they slid from rock to rock until they had a good view of what was going on in the cave. To their horror, they saw that the man who had ridden up to talk with Yuan Song at the Wise Woman's home was there with five other men. They had tied up Lao Tzu and the Robber Baron, who were sitting together with their backs against the wall of the cave. The men were armed with long swords and heavy knives. In the red light of the fire their faces were like sinister devils. All the robbers wore helmets and high boots like Yuan Song's. The flames threw their shadows on to the back wall of the cavern in flickering red and black patterns.

The young man, whom they both recognised from his woollen cloak and his dark wispy beard, was doing the talking.

"You were our leader!" he was shouting. "We trusted you, Yuan Song. You were like a father to us. Now you say we are to give back our spoils and become good citizens. You are completely crazy! What will become of us, then? Shall we not be thrown into prison, or worse?"

These were what are strictly called rhetorical questions, for neither of the two bound men could answer or speak as they had gags tied around their mouths.

"I promised you my sword between your ribs, Yuan Song, if you changed course!" yelled the young man, working himself up into a fury. "And that is what you will now get. Your friend, that big old man with the huge ears, can accompany you on your journey into the shades of night. He has nothing we can use."

So saying, the robber drew his sword and approached the poor captives who were tightly bound and utterly helpless on the cave floor.

Though Yin Hsi's hand was holding her tightly by the shoulder, Jade Fish suddenly wrenched herself free and without stopping to think ran into the cavern past the fire. The men turned round and stared at her in surprise. Several reached for their swords, thinking they were under attack.

"You bullies and cowards!" cried the girl, beside herself with rage. "Don't you dare touch these men! They are my friends. You will have to fight with me first! I am not afraid of your swords! Put them down and fight properly if you are real men!"

The idea of their having to put away their swords and fight with a young girl caused all the men to laugh out loud. Some of them looked around uncertainly at the man with the wispy beard to see how he would react.

At that moment Yin Hsi appeared in the cave mouth, lit up by the fire before him. The men, seeing his uniform, which they recognised at once as being that of one of the Border Guards, immediately drew their swords. Then they saw he was unarmed.

The young man with the wispy black beard hesitated. The girl, paying him no attention, strode over to Lao Tzu, who was lying down, bound and gagged. If you had looked really closely at him, you might have noticed that his eyes were dancing with amusement. Jade Fish stood beside him with her little fists tightly clenched at her sides. She was furious.

"Come! Are you so scared of me? I will fight with any of you!"

She put up her fists for all to see in the flickering red firelight.

It is a terrible thing to lose face and to be humiliated. It is even worse if you are supposed to be fearless robbers. The youth with the wispy beard, who seemed to be the newly self-appointed leader of this motley gang of bandits, wasn't going to risk being made a fool of by fighting, armed or unarmed, with a brave young girl. On the other hand, allowing her to taunt him and his men was equally risky. He seemed confused.

"Why are these men gagged and bound, when you have weapons and they don't?" demanded Jade Fish. "Are you so scared of what they have to say?"

"We are afraid of nobody!" said one of the other young men, a smooth-faced man with plump lips, fat jowls and very short black hair parted in the middle. He went and pulled off the cloths with which they had gagged the two men on the ground.

Immediately, the two captives started laughing, in spite of the fact that they were still tied up. Lao Tzu gave a great, low bellow of laughter. It was like hearing a bull who has been suddenly led out from a dark shed into a meadow full of brilliant, green clover. Yuan Song's shoulders shook and he guffawed until tears rolled down his cheeks. The girl still had her fists at the ready but she was disconcerted by the laughter. Were they both laughing at *her*? The gusts of laughter filled the cave like a warm, happy wind.

The wispy-bearded bandit looked totally baffled. He turned to Yin Hsi and snapped,

"What are *you* doing here, then?"

The Gatekeeper had a broad smile on his face.

"I am enjoying seeing a band of robbers defeated by one young girl, who has more bravery in her little fists than all of you put together!" And then he, too, burst out laughing.

Raucous laughter filled the dark cave.

2   It was Yuan Song, the Robber Baron, who saved the situation. He addressed the robber with the black, wispy beard, who by now was purple with humiliation and fury.

"Ling Hu," he said, when he could catch his breath again. "You don't realise it, but in capturing this old man, you have gained more riches for us than you will ever realise."

"How so?" said the young man sulkily. "I see no wealth anywhere. Speak, you ugly old man! What have you to tell us worth anything? How can you make us rich?"

Lao Tzu had finally stopped laughing. Wiping his eyes, he answered,

"A man who is happy and at peace with the world is wealthy indeed! When have any of you ever been truly happy? Can you answer me that? If you followed the right way, the Tao, then you would all have that deeper happiness and you would all be at one with yourselves, with the world and, beyond the world, you would be in tune with the whole universe."

"What is this Tao?" asked another of the men, sheathing his sword. "I've heard of the word but what does it mean? I would like to know."

"Ha! I cannot tell you straight off. The Tao that can be talked about straightforwardly is not the real Tao," answered Lao Tzu. "It is sometimes easier to talk of what the Tao is not. But before all that, these walkers here are guests of ours and they need to be fed. Go and fetch more wood for the fire and we shall make tea. Then this courageous girl will show us how to make appetising food so that we can all be friends."

There was a very long pause. All eyes turned to see how the young man, Ling Hu, would respond. He looked so fierce still, so angry with the world. Jade Fish smiled at him reassuringly, to show that she was no longer going to challenge him. Uncomfortably, Ling Hu returned her smile and he sat down, crossing his arms before his chest.

When at last they were all seated comfortably before the fire, drinking soothing tea, the bandits urged Lao Tzu to tell them more about the Tao.

"All right," he said, sipping his tea appreciatively. "Let me tell you this much about the Tao, or the Path of Virtue, as some have called it.

"If you breathe easily, if you eat well and if you sleep well, then that is a large part of the Tao and the true way of living. Nothing is to be gained from anger. Trying very hard to resolve problems usually only increases difficulties."

"Actually," continued Lao Tzu, "all this talk of mine is also bad! You don't really need an old fellow like me laying down the law! There, that is plenty enough about Tao for the moment. What we should *really* be doing is talking to each other easily, as we eat and drink."

And in a short while, that is just what they were doing. For, as wood was piled on and the fire burned up brightly, Jade Fish served them with yet more of her fine soup, this time made from two small chickens that Chan Shui had killed, plucked and packed for Jade Fish and the Gatekeeper to take with them. Into the soup went water chestnuts, bamboo shoots, curly kale, garlic, rosemary, spices and dumplings that Jade Fish showed the men how to make. Soon there were the sounds of happy laughter and lively chatter over good food, washed down with sweet-tasting mountain river water and little cups of tea.

The warm fire glowed brightly and lit up the noisy cavern.

3   In the early morning Lao Tzu rose and washed in the stream before doing his exercises. He became aware after a little while that Jade Fish was behind him, copying his movements, but soon afterwards she was joined by the Gatekeeper and seven others. There was no wind, the sun was shining and the only sound was the rushing of the stream nearby as it splashed on its downward course towards the plains and those distant palaces.

The exercises were performed with no effort and with relaxed breathing. When they Waved Hands like Clouds, the slowly drifting clouds seemed to approve. Time passed with no haste and no difficulty.

After they had all eaten together again, the robber gang prepared to return to the plains to start a newer and simpler life, following the Path of Virtue or the Tao. Before they left, Lao Tzu spoke to them briefly. While he did so, the men perched on the rocks in the sunshine and listened. He spoke for some minutes about the Tao, the Way of Perfect Virtue, which was so simple that all you had to do to follow it was to become like a child.

"We have all been children, but we forget what it is to be

like a child. In order to become strong," said Lao Tzu, "we have to become as yielding as water."

"Listen to me carefully if you wish it," he continued teasingly, "but remember always that those who say, do not know. And those who do know are those who do not say."

He paused. He smiled as he looked at their puzzled faces.

"I have already spoken too much. But think about the following, if you will. If you care about what other people think of you, you will always be their prisoner. Learn to be yourselves. Great acts are made up of little deeds. Do the complicated things while they are easy and the hard things while they are simple. A journey of a thousand miles begins with just one footstep. You can now take that small footstep along a new way, that of the mysterious Tao.

"Your way will not always be easy, but if you act with naturalness, without straining, without deliberating, you will avoid confusion. Respond intelligently, even to unintelligent treatment. Never resort to violence, even when provoked. Violence gives birth to more violence. It leads to anger, pain and unhappiness.

"Remember that the one who conquers others may be strong, but those who conquer themselves are mighty indeed. Remember also that when you are contented, you are rich beyond all measure."

Yuan Song gave Ling Hu a friendly punch on the shoulder and received a grateful whack on his back in return. They were good friends again.

Friends for *life*.

4   Lao Tzu packed his scrolls and brushes along with his bedding roll. Jade Fish and the Gatekeeper packed up all the other things and the Water Buffalo was soon strapped up with their bags. They said farewell to the seven robbers who were sitting astride their horses and ready to return to their camp in the valley to begin new lives. Ling Hu looked embarrassed again when Jade Fish gave him a friendly smile, as if to say, 'No hard feelings?'. Finally, he looked up and met her eyes. He put both his hands together and bowed his head as if to say, 'Sorry!'

"Unfortunately we cannot now steal your scrolls, Master," Yuan Song was saying, grinning. "So we shall have to learn to read so that we can later learn more about your teachings. Ling Hu will be our instructor and he has promised us knives in our ribs if we get it wrong!"

They all whooped with laughter and Ling Hu became embarrassed yet again. They turned their horses about, laughing and punching him. Then they disappeared in a clatter of hooves and a cloud of dust.

"So," said Lao Tzu cheerfully, turning back to his friends, "we are going to find the Jade Cutter who lives in the east. Is that what you tell me? Perhaps he will cut me a beautiful jade water buffalo. Are there not any number of cutters of jade in this country?"

"There is only one jeweller who made this fish," insisted Jade Fish. "Chan Shui recognised its handiwork. We must search for the Royal Jade Cutter."

They set off, taking a path that led eastward. The day was fine and as they descended towards the plains beyond the foothills the sun burned hot overhead. Everywhere they travelled, that day and the next, they showed people the green fish necklace and asked if the villagers recognised the craftwork. It was late in the evening of the third day when they struck lucky.

"Ah, yes!" said a woman who was working in a rice allotment. She had a basket on her back and was busy planting new lime-green shoots in the watery soil. "I know whose work that is. There's only one man who could make something like that. He lives up in the village, there, under that tall cliff. His name is Tan Kuo, the blind sculptor. He used to be famous but now he makes his living carving out of wood or stone for birthdays and weddings. He's very old."

Eventually they found Tan Kuo's house. It was a wooden hut right under the cliff that towered three hundred feet above his roof. He was busy in his workshop at the back, said his elderly wife, who was cooking their evening meal. She smiled a gummy smile and showed them the way across the sandy courtyard.

Tan Kuo was very old and wizened. He was working on a piece of wood that he was busy shaping into a beautiful tortoise about the size of your hand. It was made of a very hard, dark wood and already the animal looked alive. He stopped when he heard that visitors had arrived, and asked who they were. His aged face was creased with lines of worry and his hair and beard were thin and white with age.

"Lao Tzu is one of our guests," said his wife to him.

"I have heard tell of that man," said the old sculptor. He stared sightlessly with closed and deeply wrinkled eyes. He could not see, but his hands constantly worked at the piece of wood. "If you are who I think you are, Master, you are most welcome here."

"This is a girl who says you might have made her necklace," continued the woman, and she pressed into his leathery old hands the green jade carp, which Jade Fish had removed from her neck. "It is a green fish, of jade."

The old man's fingers ran over the smooth scales and contours of the fish. His anxious face creased into a smile of recognition.

"Why, yes, indeed!" he said. "I did make this piece!"

Then his smile turned to alarm as he continued to stroke the fish. "But who are you?" he muttered. "Why have you come here? This fish brought about my ruin!"

"I have come to find you, sir," said Jade Fish soothingly, "because I do not know who I am or why I possess this necklace."

"I made this fish of green jade for the warlord, Zhou Hin who was the king at the Court of the Peacock Palaces. I had strict instructions. It was to be a unique piece of jewellery and he was to give it, so it was said, to his sister-in-law, the beautiful Fan Lian, as a birthday present. When his wife, the queen, Zhou Ting found out, she was furious. She was particularly angry because her younger sister was exceedingly pretty and was admired by everybody at the court.

"The queen, Zhou Ting, is a very powerful woman, you must know. She has friends in high places. Very quickly I was told that I had to clear out and move far away from the court.

"Of course, I went straight to the king. 'Your Majesty,' I said, 'you asked me to make this piece of art, a carp made of green jade, but now I'm dismissed. How can that be?' 'I know,' said the king to me, 'but there is little to be done in this matter. Here is a bag of gold to sustain you and your family and ensure you a comfortable old age. You see, my wife has taken against you and there is nothing I can do about it. I'm very sorry.'"

"Such are the ways of the court, you see," said the Jade Cutter. "I have learned that however much they patronise you, however successful you seem to be, you should try to have as little to do with royal courts as possible. I am much happier, now, making toys for the children here and wooden sculptures that the people like, even though they do not pay me the prices I used to charge at court."

"What happened to Fan Lian?" asked Jade Fish. "How did I come to have her jewellery?"

"Ah, that I cannot tell you, for my wife and I had to leave the court the very next day," answered the old man, stroking his wrinkled chin with one hand and fingering the beautiful fish that he held in his other hand. "You are, however, most welcome to stay here tonight, my friends. My workshop is warm and comfortable. There is plenty of room for you to spread your bed rolls and you must come and share our supper. My wife is a good cook and we would be truly happy to offer you our hospitality."

5   When Jade Fish woke up the next morning she didn't follow Lao Tzu to the water pump, where he washed before he went out to the garden to do his exercises under the looming cliff. Instead

she lay and thought about the conversations she had heard at the supper table the previous evening.

Of course, they had talked about the Court of Zhou Ting and the Palaces of the Peacock Throne. Lao Tzu already knew something about life at the Court of the Peacock Throne from his time as Chief Librarian at Luoyang, near Chéng-zhōu in the eastern province of Henan. Zhou Ting's court was stately, the Jade Cutter had told them, and it was very beautifully appointed. Zhou Hin was referred to as the king, but in reality, he was merely the regent, the husband of the real monarch, who was Zhou Ting. She it was, Zhou Hin's wife, the scheming and politically wily Queen Zhou Ting, who held the throne, and the power that went with it. She had inherited the title from her Zhou mother. The Zhou dynasty had tentacles spreading everywhere and the family connections made each member of this widespread dynasty very rich and powerful. Cold, glittering and elegant, Zhou Ting was now the power occupying this particular throne.

One of their problems, however, the Jade Cutter told his guests, was that they had no children, and this made the queen even more bitter and meddlesome than she might otherwise have been.

"We, on the other hand, have two sons," Tan Lan the Jade Cutter's wife had said, bringing in platefuls of spicy, freshwater prawns with noodles and bean curd. "They both work as sculptors and carvers but they've moved further to the east. They were scared that Zhou Hin's wife would try to make trouble for them, also, if they lived too close to the royal precincts."

"The only person who could stand up to the queen was the Emissary," Tan Kuo told his guests. "Bien Manchu is an ambassador, who acts as a go-between for the court of the Peacock Throne. He is a good man. He travelled to Chéng-zhōu several times, where I think he said he met you, Master, (this to Lao Tzu) and he even, so I was told, visited the lands of Qin, the Forbidden Lands of the West, on secret missions. Bien Manchu is the man who came to me from Zhou Hin commissioned this jade fish for the king's sister-in-law, Fan Lian."

"That was before Fan Lian fell into disgrace," added Tan Lan, the old man's wife. "We heard after we left that the queen's sister was in disgrace and later had to move away."

The old man had looked sharply towards his wife before saying to their visitors,

"We know nothing about this, you understand. We don't know what she was supposed to have done, why she was sent away, or where she went. We always liked her. She was pretty and charming. Much more so than her devilish sister. But all of that is in the past. We just live quietly here and we do not wish to rake over embers which might flare up. The past is the past and now we just live in the present."

"Living in the present is a good thing to do," commented Lao Tzu.

"Master," said Tan Kuo. "I know who you are. Please accept this Water Buffalo carved in hard black wood."

His wife had reached up to a row of animals standing on a shelf in the kitchen and she drew down a black water buffalo, every bit as beautiful as Shuïniù.

"I know from my wife," the old Sculptor had said, "that you are attached to the lovely black beast you have tethered in our back yard. Tan Lan is very taken with her. Please accept this carving which I made out of ebony from southern India last year. I, too, love these animals."

"I do not usually like to burden myself with things," Lao Tzu had replied. "However, this sculpture is particularly fine. It was given from the heart and I accept it with gratitude. Perhaps the Gatekeeper and his wife could look after it for me when I depart on my travels one of these days?"

The Gatekeeper had graciously assented.

Jade Fish thought about all of this before she rose.

6   "Please tell us more about the Tao, Master Lao Tzu," Tan Lan, the sculptor's wife said as they breakfasted. A bird was singing in a cherry tree outside and his song poured in through the open window, along with the golden sunshine. "We should like to live in harmony and be less worried in our lives."

"I wrote this recently," said Lao Tzu. He recited,
'Know the white, but keep the black.
Be an example for others to follow,
True and unswerving, you can set yourself the highest ideals,
For these are timeless.
Know honour

Yet follow a humble path.
Be like the valley that receives everything into it,
For, being such a valley,
You will have the power to return
To the state of the uncarved block.
Only when a block is carved, does it become useful and valuable.
When the wise understand this,
Then they can have power to rule;
For, truly, the greatest rulers, like the best sculptors,
Are those who make the fewest cuts.'"

Tan Kuo nodded his head vigorously at this.

"I agree!" he said. "A good sculptor is not constantly chipping away at things. He knows just what has to be cut and where."

"If that is so," murmured Tan Lan smiling, "then why am I always clearing up so much mess in your workshop?"

They all laughed at that.

7 "What are your plans now?" said Tan Lan, the Jade Cutter's wife. She was busy making more noodles to go with a fine stew she was preparing with pigeon breasts, ginger, home-grown peppers and bamboo shoots.

"I must go to the Palaces of the Peacock Throne," asserted Jade Fish, "to try to find out what happened to Fan Lian. I have the jade fish that was ordered for her, so if she's still alive she might know how I came to have it and why I was put out on the hillside, either to die or to be found."

"When the Emissary, Bien Manchu, ordered me to make a green jade fish for His Highness the King," said the old Jade Cutter, "he also ordered a lion in white jade for his own son. I was sent away from the court before I could deliver it to the Emissary.

"Who knows? If you're travelling to the city of the Peacock Palaces and the Court of Zhou Ting, perhaps you will meet the Emissary on your journey. If so, I should like you to give him the sculpture for his son, if he is still living."

Tan Kuo hobbled to his workshop and returned with a beautiful little lion in white jade. It snarled and bared its teeth, but that was just the way of lions. Looking at him, you could see that not only was he beautiful, with a thick white furry ruff round his strong neck, but that he was also powerful and a friend to those he held dear. There was a placid look about the eyes, and his stance was serene. Jade Fish was intrigued and delighted with it.

"How will he pay you for it?" she asked, as Tan Kuo wrapped it in a silk cloth and handed it to her.

The Carver laughed.

"Some things do not need payment. It was many years back now and he was a good man who was unhappy working for warlords whom he could never trust. My payment will be in knowing that one day, perhaps, his son will have something fine to carry with him. I hope it will bring him and his family good luck."

8   The next day they said farewell to the elderly couple in the sunshine outside their home. Before they left the house, Tan Kuo presented the Gatekeeper with a miniature pair of gates set in an arched entrance. They were made of old ivory and Tan Kuo had stayed up all night fashioning them. Yin Hsi was very moved by this present, but Tan Kuo would accept no payment for the gift. Tan Lan held one of her husband's wrinkled hands in hers, while he stroked the back of Shuïniù the Water Buffalo with the other.

"You and your wife must then come and stay with us one day," said the Gatekeeper. "It is only a five or six-day journey and we could find plenty of work for you if you brought some of your carvings to show in the town. Many merchants from the west who trade there are after just such wonderful craftsmanship as you are master of."

"We have no need of wealth," answered Tan Kuo, "though I thank you for the thought. We should certainly like to visit your border town of which we have heard so much, but it would be for pleasure and companionship rather than for business."

"You're going north towards the Palaces of the Peacock Throne," said Tan Lan his wife pointing out the road they were to take. She then reached down to a basket at her feet and began packing up food and drink in Shuïniù's saddlebags for them to take with them on their journey.

"Be sure," she said, "to stop at the Lake of Paradise. It is on your way, and it is one of the rare beauties of the region."

Her husband nodded his head vigorously in agreement.

"I have heard tell of it," replied Lao Tzu. "I have always wanted to fish there."

They thanked the couple and set off on their way again.

9   On the second day of travelling they finally reached the broad expanses that they had seen from the mountain pass of the Steep Rocks Gorge. There the mountain rivers slowed up and became one wide river. It meandered lazily in huge sweeping bows around the wide savannahs and the well-irrigated rice fields of the flat lands in the middle of this enormous valley bowl.

One of the sweeps of the river brought them into an exotic land of marshes and there they found what Lao Tzu had been looking forward to. He had come there many, many years ago as a child, he said.

It was called the Lake of Paradise.

So great was this lake that you couldn't see the further shore unless you were prepared to climb to the tops of the tall trees that bordered the water. Masses of reeds, bulrushes and ferns grew here, sheltering ducks and geese in their thousands. Long-legged ibises and white cranes picked their way delicately around the shallows, searching for fish or interesting weeds. Herons lazily flapped and skimmed over the lapping wavelets, also searching for fish.

They passed a bright-eyed old man fishing from a boat close to the shore. He had two tame black cormorants with him. He tied a string round their necks and then sent them off to find fish. The string prevented them from swallowing the fish down their greedy gullets. Instead, when the birds returned, the elderly man would take the fish from their long beaks. Just then, one of the cormorants flew back with a large fish flapping in its long beak. The old fisherman untied the string around the bird's throat and gave it a much smaller fish, as a reward, from a bag in the boat. The second bird likewise returned with its prize, a similarly large fish. He too was rewarded by the fisherman. Then, the man turned to the three spectators on the bank and offered them the two fish that were squirming furiously at his feet.

"Now, that's an ingenious way to catch your food!" called out Yin Hsi, full of admiration. He waded over to the boat and took the two fish with thanks.

"It's how we go about it here," said the elderly fisherman smiling cheerfully. "The birds are cleverer than us at catching fish and they are good friends. We look after them and they look after us."

Shuïniù, the black Water Buffalo, was overjoyed to be allowed to wallow in the water after her bags had been removed. She drank, lay down and rolled happily in the shallow, muddy edges, while the tired travellers made a fire to cook the fish and then stretched themselves out on the sand in the shade of some wide-leafed bushes.

Some children from a nearby village came past after they had eaten. There were two small grubby-faced boys and two older and taller girls who couldn't stop smiling. They all carried fishing rods and baskets. Lao Tzu talked with them and they asked him if he would like to fish with them. There was nothing he wanted better, he answered. Jade Fish went with them to watch. The elder boy lent Lao Tzu his fishing rod and one of the beaming girls showed the big-eared giant how to tie his hooks on, and afterwards she baited each hook with a fat, juicy worm.

The girls giggled to see the vast stranger casting his line into the lake. They waited breathlessly to see what, if anything, this extraordinary old man would catch. After only a few minutes there was a tug on the line and Lao Tzu excitedly pulled in a fat carp, its gilded scales gleaming in the sunlight. The children clapped their hands in encouragement and the Master was obliged to repeat his success.

The second fish was even bigger and the children all helped him to land the gasping monster. He tried to give the larger fish to the children but they giggled shyly and refused. Finally, they accepted the lesser of the two golden carp. Lao Tzu bowed to the children and thanked them. Still laughing, they bowed back, and then they cheerfully waved goodbye and continued on their way along the shore.

"Unless you *become* like a child," said Lao Tzu, half to himself, "and see the world through the eyes of a child, you will lack the simplicity of Tao, the Way of timeless Virtue."

It was warm beside the lakeshore. They watched as three white cranes took off from the lake, flapping their wings furiously and scrabbling with their legs before gracefully taking to the reed-scented air. That evening, after they had performed their exercises before the lapping waters and the setting sun, they slept soundly. The dark, moonless sky was set ablaze with thousands of brilliant stars. The only soothing disturbances were the croaking of the frogs and hooting of the owls in the woods behind the shores of Lake Paradise.

The following day, by nightfall, they arrived at the Palaces of Zhou Ting and the Court of the Peacock Throne.

Cast away sainthood and banish wisdom;
People will be a hundred times better off;
Cast away gentility and banish strict morality,
People will rediscover compassion and human obligation.
Cast away cleverness and profit;
Bandits and thieves will disappear...
The greatest importance is to see
The raw silk of simplicity
To realise your true inner nature.
Be selfless and limit your desires.

(**Tao Tê Ching** - The Classic of the Way and Its Virtue - XIX)

PART SIX

When you counsel a ruler in the way of Tao,
Advise them against the use of force,
For that always creates resistance.
Thorns and brambles grow where an army has passed.
Wars never promote prosperity.
Never use power to gain advantage.
Achieve results,
But do not glory in them.

(**Tao Tê Ching** - The Classic of the Way and Its Virtue - XXX)

I The palaces of Zhou Ting dominated the town. In front of the three Heavenly Palaces, a lake glistened in the sunshine, but this was very different from the Lake of Paradise where they had been the day before. The lake was smaller for a start, and it was also tamer. The shore was bordered by gravel walks and by carefully trimmed weeping willows. Swans and ducks paraded on the crystal blue water, but they paddled under pretty, ornamental bridges or drifted past neatly painted pavilions and pagodas. There was a constant quacking and squawking on the water. On the banks, groups of exotic birds waddled awkwardly, patrolling and keeping watch over their families and partners.

The town faced the palaces from the opposite side of the lake. Beyond the town rolled the wide, muddy river, who had led them here and whose waters kept the artificial lake full. Much of the town's business seemed to be linked to maintaining the palaces and the royal court, but strangely there was little activity in the streets.

The travellers stopped at a tea shop that proclaimed itself as the Heavenly Peacock Palaces Tea Centre. Two beautiful girls dressed in long blue silk dresses came to serve them tea in small decorated porcelain cups. They knelt and poured the tea, which was accompanied by tiny, honeyed rice cakes.

When they were asked about the king and queen, the two girls looked astonished.

"Why, haven't you heard?" said one, pausing as she poured a thin brown stream from the fine teapot decorated with blue peacocks and regal court officials on lemon-yellow lawns. "The king and queen have both died. It all happened less than three months ago."

"The monarch, Zhou Ting, had been ill for some years," said the other, offering them rice cakes, and discreetly slipping one of them into her perfectly shaped mouth. "She died very peacefully at the end, although there had been months of rumours and turbulence in the court. Her physicians had tried everything."

"Her end was the *only* peaceful aspect of her life," interrupted the first girl slyly. "I don't think many people in the town mourned her passing."

"But Zhou Hin, the Regent, was totally distraught," continued the other girl. "He proclaimed three months of mourning and appeared at her funeral looking so haggard and wretched, poor man."

"And within three weeks, he too was dead!" concluded the first girl, pouring more tea out. "Of course, many people suspected poison, which is only natural!"

Lao Tzu laughed at this and nearly spilt his tea.

"But, you see, there were no suspicious circumstances at all, according to the Court Apothecaries," continued the first girl, unaware that she had said anything funny.

"Will you have more cakes?" asked the girl with the tray of rice cakes. "You're not from these parts, are you?"

"No," said Jade Fish. "We're looking for Zhou Ting's sister, Fan Lian."

The two serving girls exchanged looks of surprise.

"I had no idea that the queen had a sister!" muttered the first girl, as she poured out some more tea.

"What has happened to the court? Who is the ruler now?" asked Jade Fish.

"We have no ruler!" giggled the other girl offering the rice cakes around again, but this time she didn't take one for herself. "We feel much better not having a ruler. All the courtiers and palace advisors have left for the hills. Many people think they have emptied the palace coffers and have taken all the wealth for themselves."

"The palaces are practically empty!" said the first girl. "If you wish to stay here at the Tea Centre there are rooms available, but the owner charges quite a lot, I'm afraid."

Yin Hsi paid for their teas and, thanking the two pretty girls, they left.

2   The sun was setting as they circled the lake and approached the three palaces. These were three enormous red-lacquered timber pagodas, with a taller, dark red watch-tower set to one side. There were formal gardens at the front, while behind them lay a forest leading up to some low hills.

All seemed forlorn and empty as they approached. Shuïniù, the huge Water Buffalo led the way, casting an envious eye on the large ornamental lake. She would have liked to take an evening bath there but she seemed to feel this might be inappropriate, and so they pressed on through the wide stone-arched entrance leading to the palaces.

The place seemed totally deserted. Glancing around, the travellers stared in wonder at all the peacocks who were strutting or stalking over the lawns. Many were brilliant blue males spreading their magnificent fan-like tail feathers. Some were dowdier, brown or fawn females, and just three were pure white. A few screeched and cried in protest at the visitors' arrival.

The elegant gardens were carefully groomed, with flowering rhododendrons, azaleas, orange blossom bushes and masses of brightly coloured peonies. These would probably have come from Luoyang, said Lao Tzu knowledgeably. An elderly gardener stopped working at a bed of flowers and stared at them in surprise.

"Are you connected with the Court, my good sirs?" he asked them. "There's nobody left there any more. They've all gone."

"Who pays your wages now?" asked Lao Tzu curiously. "Are you the only person here?"

The aged gardener laughed and rested on his spade, stroking his thin beard. He removed his wide straw hat and wiped his brow with a red kerchief.

"We hardly need wages here, sir. We grow everything we need and more. No, my masters, I'm not the only person here. Some of the servants have stayed on. The Palaces have to be looked after and protected by somebody, don't they?"

They found a side door that was not barred and entered the largest palace, which was set in the middle of the gardens. The wooden halls, dark and silent, were all empty. The visitors' footsteps echoed on the vast polished flagstones. They climbed the wide, red-painted wooden staircase that led to the royal chambers above. Glossy, red-lacquered walls were carved and intricately ornamented with gold. Tasselled silk hangings showed hunting scenes. Bronze swords and painted spears hung in decorative clusters.

Full of curiosity they moved from hall to hall. In the last room, an antechamber next to the queen's own bedroom, they found a very old woman seated in a tall, bamboo armchair with silk cushions of dark green. She was thin and deeply wrinkled but she held herself straight and turned her head to try to see who these newcomers could be. Her pale eyes were clouded with age.

"Who are you, madam?" asked Lao Tzu gently, after he had apologised for their intrusion.

"I am Mu Ju," said the ancient woman. "I used to be Nurse to the Royal Household, but since they have all gone I'm no longer a nurse to anybody."

"You must have known the royal family well," said Jade Fish curiously, coming close to her and immediately taking one of her hands to stroke.

"Ah, a young girl," replied the old woman calmly, allowing her hand to be gently caressed. "My dear, your voice reminds me of somebody...

"Yes, I was lucky to have been kept on for so long, since I'm very old and I no longer see well. The queen wanted to get rid of me, for she never had children and she resented my being here, especially as I had a child to look after, a lovely girl called Li Po. She was my grand-daughter, whom I cared for after her mother, my own poor daughter, tragically died. Luckily the Regent, Zhou Hin, wouldn't hear of my being sent away."

"That must have been welcome news for all living here," said Lao Tzu, "for I know you, madam, and I know you once had an excellent reputation in the imperial court of Chéng-zhōu."

"Who are you, sir?" she asked wonderingly. "You have a deep voice that I recognise. I was once at Luoyang, where I heard Lao Tzu talk in the Royal Libraries. He spoke of the

Tao, but that was in the days when I was young and a wet nurse to the children of the Empress at Chéng-zhōu nearby."

"I remember the occasion well," said Lao Tzu. He laughed. " I think, Mu Ju, that you were one of the few people there who was really interested in what I had to say. Where is your grand-daughter now, madam?"

"Ah, sir, if only I knew, I should be so happy," said Mu Ju, sadly. "She left suddenly at the time when the queen's young sister fell into disgrace. Fan Lian and Li Po my grand-daughter were close friends. When Fan Lian disappeared one day, so too did my very dear grand-daughter and I've never heard a word from her since. It was as if she had died."

Jade Fish's hands reached up to her neck and unfastening her pendant she said,

"Madam, do you know this?"

Into the old woman's wrinkled hands she pressed the green fish made of jade.

3 The woman inspected the carving carefully, holding it up closely to her misty eyes. As her gnarled hands turned the object over slowly, and as they carefully felt the smooth scales, the fins and the tail, her face broke into an amazed smile of recognition.

"The jade fish! It was made for Fan Lian! That girl was herself a treasure even though she fell into disgrace. How did you come by this, my girl?"

"That is what I have come to try to discover, madam," answered Jade Fish. "Wasn't it given to the queen's sister, Fan Lian?"

"Fan Lian had no children," murmured the old woman. "Before she left, she had to return this present to Zhou Hin, who had created such a stir by giving it to her in the first place. I was present when the Emissary, Bien Manchu, returned with it. The king was terribly angry. For days he was went stamping around the palace so that I thought the floorboards were going to break. Even the queen was scared, which is saying a great deal given her own bad temper.

"Of course, we all knew the truth. The truth was that the king was half in love with Fan Lian, even though she was in disgrace for something or other. Zhou Ting, the queen, was utterly enraged that her husband should have given her sister such a beautiful necklace. She wanted it destroyed at once."

"But, madam, why was Fan Lian in disgrace?" asked Jade Fish. "What had she done wrong?"

"Ah, now that I cannot tell you, nor, I think, will we ever know now," replied the old woman, still stroking the fish lovingly. "There was plenty of gossip and speculation here at the court, as you might imagine, but nobody ever knew what the story was. The only person who might have known was the Emissary. He was a most reputable gentleman and he commanded respect from everybody. But, sadly he passed away with a fever he contracted after one of his journeys to the Court of the Qin in the west, only two years ago. He was trying to negotiate an agreement between Zhou Ting and the Warlords of Qin."

"I heard of that mission, Mu Ju," said Lao Tzu, pulling at one of his enormous ears and nodding his big head. "I didn't know that Counsellor Bien Manchu had died. He was a good man, as you rightly say."

"So, my girl," said Mu Ju, handing back the precious necklace, "unless you stole this jewel from the king himself, which is not very likely, I am at a loss to explain how it came into your possession."

Jade Fish told the old woman how she had been left on the hillside in a rich shawl with the necklace. Mu Ju listened keenly but she had no idea what could have happened.

"I knew that shawl from my nursing days. I often wondered what became of it. You are welcome to stay here. There are so many empty bedrooms now in the palaces. The cook and some of the servants stayed on, so the food will be excellent. The vegetables come straight from the palace gardens. I shall be pleased to have company. Perhaps in your search for Fan Lian you might come across news of my grand-daughter, Li Po. I should so like to hear from her."

The old woman's cloudy eyes filled with tears which she wiped away with a cotton handkerchief, embroidered with dark red roses.

4 "Where is your husband, madam?" asked Yin Hsi, who had been listening intently to the old Nurse's story. Lao Tzu, too, had been listening, but he had also been wandering around the room looking at scrolls, studying pictures and picking up objects on the shelves: porcelain bowls, wooden caskets and small ivory statuettes.

"My poor husband is the reason why I am here and not in Chéng-zhōu," replied Mu Ju. "He was posted here from Luoyang to be in the royal guards. He was a very brave and popular captain of the guards and people said that he might have become a general in time, but he died in an ambush at one of the northern border lookout posts. It was a band of Qin soldiers who were trying to infiltrate the territory."

"Life must be hard for you if you have difficulty seeing, your employers are dead, and all your friends and family have disappeared," said Lao Tzu studying the portrait of a warrior king on horseback.

"There are times, sir, when that is true," said the old Nurse, smiling gently. "But I manage all right. Here I am looked after and I have my sweet old cat Bài Mâo for company."

A white cat in a basket on the floor stretched itself on hearing its name and strolled over to be introduced.

"The servants are good friends," she continued, reaching down to stroke Bài Mâo's ears, "and I've had a happy life on the whole. I attended to your lecture, sir, about the Way of Tao, and I've tried to put some of those ideas into practice in my own life. My only regret in this world is that I have no news of my grand-daughter, Li Po. I brought her up as my daughter when her mother, my own poor daughter, died. I should simply like to know if she is alive or dead."

That evening the visitors spread their rolls in two of the Guest Apartments. Jade Fish was in the one which the disgraced Fan Lian had used, and the two men shared another, next door. Fan Lian's bedchamber offered no clues to her whereabouts. It was a simple room with dark, wooden furniture. Only the rich, silken bed coverings, of deep reds and jade greens, gave any clue as to her tastes.

Before they retired, they were treated to a generous banquet of pork from the royal sties, baked with artichokes, sweet onions, ginger and peas, all from the palace gardens and hothouses. The old gardener ate with them, along with a few elderly servants. There was plenty of chat and laughter while they gossiped and remembered stories of the past.

There was much interest, too, in the enormous old stranger with the huge ears, for Mu Ju had told the dining company of his wisdom and his knowledge of the Tao. They urged him to speak, in spite of Lao Tzu's protests. He told them he had no real knowledge to impart, merely a few simple ideas which might sound somewhat contradictory at times. The old servants disagreed when they heard some of what he had to say. To them the Tao made perfect sense.

Later, Jade Fish sat on her balcony long after night had fallen. Before she went to bed, she stared out at the darkened lake and the dim flickerings of firelight from the invisible town beyond. She had been surprised by the old Gardener, who had seemed uneasy when she talked to him. It was almost as if he were scared of her. She wondered if she had said something wrong.

Her thoughts then turned to Fan Lian and she wondered yet again where the queen's sister might be, if she were still alive. She pondered why and how the mysterious green fish, which Fan Lian must have worn in this very same room, had passed to her, Jade Fish, Yu Yù.

She searched the large room with its painted cupboards and carved cabinets, but she could find no clues whatsoever.

5   In the morning, Lao Tzu disappeared towards the library so that he could continue with his writing. Yin Hsi went to discuss horticultural matters in the gardens near the ornamental lake with the elderly gardener. Jade Fish, meanwhile, took the opportunity to sit and talk further with the Nurse, Mu Ju, in the royal nurseries. The apartment was sad, with no traces of children, no toys, no cots, nor any clothing. She held the old lady's hands, stroking them gently, and asked about her childhood in Luoyang.

"Ah, that was so long ago," replied Mu Ju the Nurse wistfully. "My brothers and I used to run errands for the courtiers. Our father was a servant at the court in Chéng-zhōu, but a superior servant, a chamberlain. He could be trusted with secrets, and was sometimes sent on journeys to deliver important messages. I remember, once, he took me with him on a journey where we went on a boat on a river. I forget which, perhaps it was the great Yellow River. It was as wide as an ocean. It was all so strange and exciting and I loved having my father all to myself for once."

"That must have been wonderful," said Jade Fish wistfully.

"I would so like to have had parents while I was growing up, and a grandmother like you!"

"You can have me any time," laughed Mu Ju, "for what I'm worth. Nowadays that is not much."

"Tell me more about Fan Lian," said Jade Fish. "What was she like? Why did she just disappear like that?"

"Fan Lian was a lovely little girl," replied the Nurse. "I looked after her and her sister, Zhou Ting. Zhou Ting was older and bossy with all who crossed her path, whereas Fan Lian was charming to everyone. She used to skip everywhere, singing and telling stories, to me, to the dogs, to her dolls. She was attractive and people loved her.

"Later on the Regent, Zhou Ting's husband, who liked to be referred to as the King, developed a soft spot for Fan Lian, his wife's younger sister, which I think drove Zhou Ting wild. This jade fish you wear was ordered specially for Fan Lian's birthday. I remember the Jade Cutter was given special instructions."

Jade Fish told the woman how they had met the Jade Cutter and his wife.

"He mentioned that he had made a white lion for the Emissary's son," she said.

"I know nothing about that," replied Mu Ju. "I know only that the queen was furious when the jade fish was presented to Fan Lian. But that was not why Fan Lian left. There was some other disgrace which was kept from everybody. Only the Emissary knew about such matters. I would see Zhou Hin and the Emissary talking gravely on the veranda, while Zhou Ting sulked in her chamber.

"Then, one day Fan Lian simply disappeared, along with Li Po, my grand-daughter, who was her friend and chambermaid. When we asked where they were, we were told that the king had sent Fan Lian away and she was not to be talked of any more. Zhou Ting seemed pleased and life returned to normal after that. We were heartbroken, however. It was like hearing of two deaths. We were left wondering what could possibly have happened to the girls and where they could be. Nobody knew anything."

6   Lao Tzu talked at dinner to Mu Ju, the cook and the servants about his work that day. He seemed pleased with his progress but said that it was the by far the hardest task of his long and very uneventful life.

"The Tao is simple," he said, "but writing about the Tao is extremely hard. A good solution would be to write very little. The best solution would be not to write anything at all!"

He burst out laughing.

"You must know," he continued, speaking to the cook, who was a round-faced woman with plump, red cheeks, "this chicken is delicious, but if it were served with too many ingredients and cooked for too long it would be utterly ruined. I was thinking about cooking just this afternoon in my writing."

"   Is it a recipe, sir?" asked the Cook. "I like to collect new recipes."

"It is more like a recipe for rulers," said Lao Tzu happily, his sharp, brown eyes sparkling with amusement. "May I quote it to you?"

"Most certainly, sir," replied the Cook, serving him with noodles and cashew nuts, stir-fried with fresh peppers, garlic and baby cucumbers, in a sweet soya sauce.

"'Ruling a country is like cooking a small fish.
Knowing your way in the universe
And having Tao with you for company,
You leave evil no power to do harm.'"

The Cook smiled at the Master.

"Perhaps you would like me to rule the country," she said, and then they both roared with laughter.

"At least nobody would go hungry," she added.

They all tucked into the food and for a few minutes the conversations paused.

"Is the Tao just for rulers, then, for queens and kings like Zhou Ting and Zhou Hin," asked the elderly Gardener after a while, "or is it for ordinary people like us as well?"

Lao Tzu laughed contentedly again and helped himself to more of the delicious chicken and noodles from the large earthenware pot.

"We are all ordinary," he observed. "Is it so extraordinary to be born, to learn, to raise children, to grow old and to die? Why should the Way of Virtue and Happiness not apply to everybody? It is because it applies to everyone that it is so important for rulers to take note of it."

"Can you tell us more, Master?" asked the Cook. "Tell us your recipes for living well and perhaps I shall share mine with you for eating well!"

"I shall tell you, then, more of what I wrote this afternoon in the peace of the royal library," answered Lao Tzu putting down his bowl and wiping his fingers carefully.

"The wisest make no judgments of their own;
They follow the hearts of ordinary people.
They are good to people who are good
And they are good to people who are not good.
Goodness is its own virtue.

They believe truthful people,
But they also believe the liars,
Because truth resides in having faith in everybody.
The wisest therefore reserve judgment,
Even seeming confused at times
In their dealings with the world.
Let others strain their eyes and ears;
The wisest look and listen just like a little child."

"I like that," said Mu Ju, the Nurse. "As you know, I have always loved little children."

7   "The Emissary, Bien Manchu, did have a son, didn't he?" Jade Fish asked Mu Ju before going to her bedroom to sleep that night.

"Yes, my dear," answered the aged woman, who was enjoying having a young girl to talk to once more. "He would be a year or two older than you, I would think. Bien Jin was a clever, warm-hearted boy. The king was much taken with him. The Emissary's widow, however, moved back to the east with him and his sister when her husband died. We were sorry to see the family depart. Who knows where they all are? Everybody has left and there's no ruler now. The Peacock Throne is empty."

"Is there really a Peacock Throne?" asked Jade Fish.

"Have you not been to see it yet?" replied the Nurse, surprised. "You must ask the Gardener to show you. It's well worth the visit. I would offer to take you, but I stumble now and don't see so well."

The Gardener, looking a little wary, offered to take the girl to see the Peacock Throne that afternoon. It occupied the whole of the smallest of the three palaces. It was like a small cathedral inside, dark and musty, for it had not been used for several months. The Gardener began lighting many small oil lamps along the walls. Jade Fish helped him and at last one hundred and eight little flames were flickering and lighting up the vast hall. The ancient wooden walls were richly decorated with painted peacocks, of course. Brilliantly coloured in blues and greens, or else sculpted in white wood, peacocks everywhere perched and strutted.

There in the middle was the most elaborate of thrones.

The seat was painted in gold, but the tall arms of the enormous throne were shaped like peacock wings and the high back was a resplendent fan made up of carved wooden feathers in blue and green just like a real peacock's tail, only, of course, far bigger.

Jade Fish wanted to go and sit in the seat but the Gardener stopped her.

"Only the ruler may sit there," he said a triflr sternly.

"But there *is* no ruler," objected Jade Fish smiling.

She didn't want to offend the elderly man who still seemed uneasy in her presence, so instead she walked all round it, staring at the dazzling colours and the intricate carving.

8   For the next three days Jade Fish saw little of the Master, who was in the library each day with his ink bowl and brushes, busily writing. In the mornings, she led the Nurse into the gardens where they walked or sat in the sunshine by the Palace Lake. They talked continuously and Mu Ju enjoyed telling the girl about the past - a past of wars and warriors, when life at court was more turbulent and unforeseeable. There was mixed happiness and pain in nearly all of her stories. Jade Fish thought that perhaps this was the way most old people, people who had lived through so much, both good and bad, remembered the olden times.

At the end of the third day she visited Lao Tzu in the library.

"So, Jade Fish has come to disturb me," boomed the huge old man, looking up cheerfully from the vertical strip of bamboo he was busy working on. The painted brushwork looked beautiful to the girl as the inky characters snaked their way down the bamboo strips in delicate flowing lines. They seemed like falling leaves or ivy trailing down a tree trunk. It suddenly came to her that she, too, wanted to write and read like that. More than anything else in the world.

The library was light and airy, with large tables where you could unroll a scroll and read or write at your leisure. The walls were lined with shelves on which were stacked rolls and rolls of documents on thin slips of bamboo. Paintings covered the spaces where there were no shelves. Large windows let in light from three sides and there were views out over the lake to the south and the hills and mountains stretching further back along the route where they had travelled.

"I've spent most of my life in such libraries, my girl, poring over state documents, memoirs, poems, histories and letters. And all to what end?"

The Master sighed and smiled at Jade Fish.

"Don't be tempted yourself to seek fulfilment in libraries," he cautioned. "I fear I'm writing just another such document to clutter up people's brains, when, instead of reading such stuff, they should be *living* their lives and engaging in fuller pursuits."

"Master, I want to read and write properly, so that I can *know* more and lead a fuller life. The choice will be mine what I read or write, but at least it will be *my* choice, surely?"

"You're probably right, Jade Fish," chuckled Lao Tzu. "Shall I show you what I have written today? You learn quickly. You'll probably be writing your own memoirs next week!"

And he gave one of his customary bellows of laughter. He told her that he was almost at the end.

"What will happen then?" asked the girl alarmed.

"Why, then it will be time for me to move on," he said,

unperturbed. "Yin Hsi must be returning to his wife and his duties. You have your life to lead. And I shall depart to the west, seeking silence and solitude in my old age."

"But you can't leave us!" cried the girl, suddenly sensing a wave of disquiet taking hold of her.

"All things must come to an end," announced Lao Tzu imperturbably, taking her hands and regarding her calmly. "Endings are not to be feared. They form part of our natural course. We have beginnings and we have endings. Accepting these with serenity is an important part in following the path of wisdom."

Together they examined what Lao Tzu had written that afternoon and he showed her what each character signified and how it had been formed.

9   *'True words are not full of beauty;*
Beautiful words are not full of truth.
Good people will not prove goodness by sophisticated arguments,
Nor are those who prove things by arguments alone necessarily
good people.
True knowledge is different from deep learning:
Deep learning in itself doesn't lead to wisdom.

The wise have no need to store things up.
The more that they use up for others, the more they have;
The more that they give to others, the more they acquire.

The Tao of Heaven sharpens without cutting:
The Tao of the wise is to work without striving.'

"To think," muttered Lao Tzu, his big belly already beginning to rumble with laughter, "that after a lifetime spent poring over dull documents, travelling all over the country and speaking with the wisest in the land - to think that I have little more to offer than these!"

He pointed at the bamboo strips laid out before him and his wide shoulders shook with amusement.

"Perhaps people won't read these, and perhaps, too, that will not be a bad thing."

He looked at Jade Fish and his aged face creased up into a happy grin.

The Gardener outside, raking gravel in the courtyard below, was very surprised to hear waves of laughter suddenly drifting down from the library. There were high-pitched giggles and deep, growling guffaws that were like thunder reverberating around high cliffs. Together the two sounds floated out of the window and spread about the palace courtyard below.

"What can be amusing them so much amongst all those dreary, dust-covered scrolls?" the Gardener wondered to himself.

Learning is acquired by adding to one's store of knowledge day by day:

Tao is acquired by subtracting from one's store day by day.

You end up with less and less,

Until inactivity is gained.

When nothing is done, nothing is left undone.

Allow all things to take their course;

Nothing is gained by interference.

(**Tao Tê Ching** - The Classic of the Way and Its Virtue - XLVIII)

PART SEVEN

Precious things impede people and lead them astray.
Therefore the wisest consult their hearts rather than their eyes.
They consider the inner rather than the outer.

(**Tao Tê Ching** - The Classic of the Way and Its Virtue - XII)

I Before supper, Jade Fish decided to give Shuïniù a treat. She untied the huge water buffalo, who had been standing uncomfortably in the sun, chewing at the hay that had been left out for her. Then the girl led the great beast to the large ornamental lake. The graceful swans watched in some surprise as the girl, dressed in her dark cotton trousers and brown cotton shirt, stepped off the paved walkway into the shallow water and called for Shuïniù to follow her.

The black buffalo awkwardly lowered herself into the water and then delightedly rolled and sluiced herself over with cool water. Jade Fish swam towards the middle. Swimming was something the shepherds had taught her as a little girl in the pools and streams nearby.

The Gardener called to her from the lakeside where he had come running in alarm.

"You cannot swim here! It is forbidden!"

Lao Tzu also appeared, as if by magic. He laughed when he saw his water buffalo and the girl in the water.

"Why should you stop them, my friend?" he inquired gently. "They're doing no harm and anyway, the people who made these unnecessary rules are gone. It's a hot day, Gardener. Put down your rake and let's join them in the lake."

The Gardener looked very doubtful, but when he saw Lao Tzu step into the deliciously inviting water and splash water over his head and shoulders, he followed the old man in. Soon both men were sprawling in the water near the buffalo. The Gardener was soon laughing, while the Master sloshed water everywhere as he floated on his back.

"I never thought when I was younger that I would ever be doing something like this," the Gardener confided to the pair of bathers. "It's against all the old regulations, but somehow it feels very good."

2   It was during the supper of onion soup with kale and crayfish dumplings that Lao Tzu announced that he would be making his way back with Yin Hsi to the Border Town the next day.

"I've finished my writing," he said. "Yin Hsi will look after the rolls for whoever might be interested. My work is done and it's time for us to leave. The wildernesses of the west are where I will wander until such time as I stop. I shall have Shuïniù to look after me."

Jade Fish accidentally knocked her soup bowl on the marble floor.

"No!" she shouted in dismay, and ran and buried her head in the old man's rough jerkin. "You can't leave us! I need you! You said you would look after me!"

"So I did," replied the Master calmly. "But not for ever! There's no more I can do to find your parents and you will be fine here with Mu Ju and these good people to look after you. Perhaps tomorrow you will find more answers to your questions, but who knows? Stop searching and you are more likely to find."

"But I don't want to lose you!" sobbed the girl. "I don't have many friends in this world and… you and Yin Hsi have become like parents for me."

The poor girl could not look up she was crying so much.

"But you have your own way to make in this world, Yu Yù, and we too have our own ways to make," said Lao Tzu gently, stroking her head. "You're a strong girl. You would hardly wish to be stuck with an ugly old giant with big ears for very long, would you?"

"Yes, I would!" shouted the girl defiantly from within the folds of the ugly old giant's jerkin. "You are the best teacher I've ever had. And… I never had a proper one before you, even though you're… you're *improper!*"

They all had to laugh at that, including Jade Fish through her tears.

3   They were all seated at the table after Mu Ju had wiped the poor gir's face and Jade Fish had then gone and cleared up the spilt

soup. She came back and sat on the cushion where she had been sitting before. Suddenly, there was a thunder of hooves outside!

"Oh, no!" shouted the old Gardener, who had rushed to the window. "It's a gang of bandits! They've surely come to murder us and rob the palaces. We have no time to hide!"

"What can they steal that we have such need of?" scoffed Mu Ju. "They're welcome to have whatever they want. They have no right to rob or to hurt anybody, though."

Jade Fish had an idea who it might be and she was right.

Presently, in strode a handsome man with a tanned, weather-beaten face, bushy eyebrows and long, grizzled hair under his leather helmet. Behind him marched six other men, looking alert, fit and fearless. They lined up behind their leader, all in thick leather jerkins and fur boots. But, surprisingly, not one man seemed to carry a sword or weapon of any sort.

It was the Robber Baron, Yuan Song. He no longer looked angry. On the contrary, he looked happy and relaxed.

"Master," he said, addressing Lao Tzu, "I've come with my followers. I wish to thank you and to make a present of these men and myself. We have all forsworn violence and robbery. We have returned all the goods we stole, and we have received some honour already. They've been asking in the town if we could be chosen to become soldiers in the Border Force.

"My men wished to see you again and I knew you would be heading this way. We now wish to protect our countrymen and to practise your teachings and spread them. The way of the Tao is...."

"Is what?" challenged Lao Tzu, smiling. "If you can say what it is you are a far cleverer man than me!"

"There, you see!" laughed Yuan Song to his men. "I told you the Way of Tao wasn't easy. We have been busy trying to follow it, but now our Master wants us to teach him what it is!"

"Weren't you going to get *rid* of your leader?" asked the Master teasingly, addressing Ling Hu, the young man with long, black hair and the wispy beard. "You missed your opportunity. He will not make your lives easy now, following the Path of Tao!"

Lao Tzu hooted with laughter and Ling Hu looked ashamed. Nevertheless, he spoke up and his voice was clear.

"We were afraid, back then. Afraid of change, afraid of being thought unmanly, afraid of society. I was afraid to lose face. All that has changed now. Thank you, Master, for giving us back our self-respect."

"You see," said Lao Tzu chuckling to Jade Fish, "when bandits start thanking you, you *know* it's time to depart!"

Of course, this caused Jade Fish to start sobbing again. Although she tried very hard to control her sadness, she couldn't contain her tears at the thought that she was going to lose her Master and her friend.

"What's the problem?" asked Yuan Song concerned. "Can we be of any assistance?"

Yin Hsi briefly explained the situation, saying that he needed to return to oversee the Gates and that Lao Tzu's written work was finished.

"Then it is quite clear," stated the reformed Robber Baron. "My men and I will stay and we shall look after you and try to help you to find out who you are."

"Thank you, sir," said Jade Fish, smiling through her tears. "I am fortunate indeed to have so many people ready to assist me. Believe me, it makes me feel very humble. From the bottom of my heart, I thank you all."

4   Early next morning, the Master was doing his exercises in front of the lake before the sun began to rise. His arms rose and fell gently, describing circles slowly, pushing here and withdrawing softly there; his great frame moved lightly and fluently on his sturdy legs.

As before, he became aware that the girl was standing just behind him, copying his movements delicately and lightly, in perfect time with his. They continued together as the birds sang about them and blue wavelets lapped at the shore. At the end they paused for a minute or two in silence.

"You see," said Lao Tzu quietly. "You can do it all by yourself now. You don't need me any more, little Yu Yù."

"I shall always need you and I shall miss you terribly, Master," replied the girl in subdued tones, "but I hope I can learn to bear your departure."

"All departures need courage," murmured Lao Tzu, "but that is part of what it is to be human, learning to face changes. What I have said and written will always be a part of you now."

The girl ran to him and buried her face in his ample stomach. He reached his huge arms around her and hugged her gently.

"Come," he said to the weeping girl, "dry your eyes. You're a good, brave girl and you will do well in your life. It's only just beginning. You have to manage your 'Return'. All will be well. I have my own Way to manage too, old though I am."

"But you are abandoning me!" she cried out in her sadness.

"Not at all," said the old man, his bright eyes sparkling with mischief. "I'm giving you your passport to a new life."

5   After everyone had eaten together, Lao Tzu and Yin Hsi left the palace together with the black water buffalo ambling along beside them,. They were waved off at the gates by the Cook, the Gardener, Mu Ju, the other servants and the bandit gang. Only Jade Fish was missing. She had said her sad farewells but in the end she couldn't bear to watch the departure, and instead she went walking off behind the palaces.

Unlike the gardens at the front which were kept neat and well-trimmed, those at the back were wild and luxuriant and led into a forested area that rose towards some low hills. Here, there was hibiscus and frangipani. Flame trees dangled their scarlet flowers and tall white magnolia trees blossomed with waxy white flowers looking like gloved hands. Massive trees loomed overhead with lianas dangling. Chattering monkeys swung through the branches. The paths had become overgrown with thick grasses, spongy ferns and mosses. Normally the girl would have been fascinated by the strangely shaped flowers, their thick perfumes and their brilliant colours. She would have enjoyed watching the monkeys playing and quarrelling in the high trees. Today, however, she was upset and needed time to think about everything that was happening.

After nearly an hour of pushing through the undergrowth, going deeper and deeper into what had by then become a thick jungle, Jade Fish wanted to turn back. It was as she tried to retrace her steps that she realised that she had absolutely no idea where she was.

She was totally lost.

6   She tried several gaps in the undergrowth calling out loudly as she did so, but the gaps never turned into paths and she was forced to turn round. The sun had gone in so there was no clue as to which direction she should be heading in. Instead the noises in the forest grew louder if anything. Green parrots squawked and orange macaws cried to each other, echoing in the treetops. Monkeys appeared to be chattering and laughing at her plight. The rasping sound of cicadas seemed to fill the jungle.

Then something really terrible happened.

A small clearing had opened up in front of her when suddenly, as she staggered into it from the dense undergrowth, a snake reared up, hissing fiercely. It had a dark shiny body and its flattened head was framed by a wide hood. The hood had strange white markings, rather like two horse's hooves joined by a whitish bar. Being young and feeling menaced, the snake was doubly aggressive.

It happened to be the deadliest snake of all, a cobra, angry at being disturbed. Its black beady eyes fixed on the girl intently. Jade Fish froze and for a few seconds the two of them faced each other in silent watchfulness.

The snake, however, must have decided that the human represented too much of a threat, for suddenly it attacked. Lowering its head, it slithered forward, darting swiftly towards the girl's legs.

A second later Jade Fish saw the snake disappearing back into the thick foliage in front of her. Looking down at her left leg she saw two little pinpricks of blood. It was then that she felt the sharp pain.

The forest began to spin about her head.

7   Back at the palaces, Jade Fish's absence had been noticed, of course, but Mu Ju had said,

"The poor girl's upset. She's probably gone for a walk alone to help her feel better."

Yuan Song and his followers were wandering around the palaces with Mu Ju, admiring the artistry and the craftsmanship of the buildings and their costly contents.

"Sir," said the young man with the wispy beard, "let me go and see if she is all right."

"No, Ling Hu," replied the Robber Baron. "She'll be fine. The girl is moody, perhaps, and she probably needs time to be on her own."

"That's right," interjected the old Nurse. "Jade Fish can take care of herself, have no fear."

So they continued on their tour.

But Ling Hu seemed worried and he went over and asked the Gardener,

"Have you seen Jade Fish?"

"She went to the gardens round the back of the palaces," he answered. "We don't go there much. They've been left in a state of wildness."

Ling Hu went round to the back and gazed at the jungle of trees and shrubs which towered up towards the clouds. It so happened that he had been brought up in a remote village where tracking animals was commonplace. He stood still and stared carefully at the high wall of bushes and trees. His eyes saw immediately where the girl had gone: a footprint here, a bent or broken plant-stem there. Twigs had been snapped in some places and grasses trodden in others. His watchful eyes guided him through the thick undergrowth. He called as he went, but the only answer was the chirruping and screeching of birds, insects and animals. The sounds echoed round the lush jungle.

The scents were heavy: sometimes honeyed and almost sickly-sweet, sometimes sharp and pungent, like rotting vegetation or stinking mushrooms.

Half an hour later, Ling Hu found the lifeless body of the girl where she had fallen, just at the edge of the clearing. Instantly, he saw the specks of blood on her leg. Her eyes were closed. He wasn't sure if the girl was still breathing. She seemed to have no pulse either.

8   It was early afternoon and the sun was still high when the bandits saw Ling Hu carrying the body of Jade Fish into the palace where they were all staying.

"Quick!" he said. "She's been bitten by a snake. We must find a herbalist. I have tied a strap round her leg, but the poison will still be travelling to her heart."

The girl's left leg had a strap tied tightly just above her knee.

Mu Ju said, "There's a good herbalist in the town. I will have to take you to her, for you will never find the place."

Ling Hu and Yuan Song took turns carrying the girl and Mu Ju came with them. Mu Ju hurried as fast as her aged legs would carry her. A small, unknown boy from nowhere came forward to help her and lead her by the hand. They hurried as fast as they could, up stone steps and down narrow alleys. The girl was barely breathing and her respiration seemed light and irregular. She was completely unconscious.

Finally, they arrived at a small stone dwelling set among a cluster of small homes.

Nang Soo Chong, the Herbalist, slender and dainty, came to the door of her house. She was middle-aged with fine cheekbones. The woman felt the girl's pulse and immediately asked Ling Hu whether he had seen the snake. He shook his head.

They laid the girl's body carefully on a bed in the middle of the main room. All around were earthenware jars and bright porcelain pots. The little boy quickly kissed Mu Ju's wrinkled hand and then disappeared before he could be thanked. They never saw him again.

"Well," said the Herbalist calmly, "I will assume that it's a cobra. The serum will not harm her if it is another snake, but we have to act quickly. I only hope we are not too late."

She reached for one of the glazed pots on the shelf behind her and asked Mu Ju to start massaging the girl's chest above her heart while she prepared the serum. She looked grave and the men were worried. The girl's breath came and went, sometimes in harsh bursts. Sometimes there was a pause before she breathed again.

"Will she be all right?" asked Yuan Song.

"I cannot say," replied the Herbalist, stirring the pot with a stick.

The sun streamed into the room from the west as the golden afternoon turned to early evening.

9 Several hours had passed when into the Herbalist's bedroom there stole a boy on tiptoe. He was about fourteen or fifteen with dark eyes and very dark hair cropped short. He was tall, good looking and sturdy for his age, with a gentle look on his face. He bent over the still body of the girl.

Jade Fish opened one eye and then the other. She stared up at the boy in total confusion.

"Where am I? Who are you? What's happening," she murmured, still only half-awake.

"How are you feeling?" said the boy. "I am Bien Jin. I am staying with Nang Soo Chong, who's a friend of my family."

"You are Bien Jin?" gasped the girl, suddenly wide awake. "Why, you have to be be the Emissary's son."

"Correct," said the boy, smiling. "You must be mending fast if you can work out who I am. Now my question to you is, who are *you*?"

"I have no idea," said the girl, smiling back faintly. She struggled to sit up, but the effort was too much and she sank back into the pillow that was behind her head. And she fell fast asleep again.

All things in nature, animals and man,
Are born soft and weak;
But when they die they are stiff and hard.
Plants and trees are green and tender,
Filled with sweet sap when young;
But at their death they are brittle and dry.

Therefore the rigid and inflexible are the agents of death
Whereas the gentle and yielding are the agents of life...

(Tao Tê Ching - The Classic of the Way and Its Virtue - LXXVI)

PART EIGHT

My words are easy to understand and easy to put into practice,
But nobody beneath heaven comprehends or puts them into practice.
However, my words have ancient authority and a noble lineage,
And, because people don't understand this, they don't understand me.
Because so few understand me, it works to my advantage,
For I am underrated and not seen as a threat.
Therefore the sage wears rough clothes,
But he keeps a jade jewel underneath,
Next to his heart.

(**Tao Tê Ching** - The Classic of the Way and Its Virtue - LXX)

I   When Jade Fish woke again, the Herbalist was there beside her and she made the girl sip a cup of warm ginger tea with lemon and honey. The boy had disappeared.

"You've slept for two days," she said. "At one time we thought we had lost you, but you are a very strong-willed girl and you fought hard against the poison of the snake."

"Ah, the cobra! I remember now," said Jade Fish weakly. Her throat felt sore, her lungs ached and her leg hurt her. "Did you give me medicines to help fight it? Who found me? Who was that boy...? Where is he? Where am I?"

"That's far too many questions for somebody who has just returned from the edge of the dark lands," laughed Nang Soo Chong. "The boy is staying with me. I know his family well."

"The Emissary's son, Bien Jin?" asked Jade Fish eagerly. She sipped her tea, which felt very soothing for her throat.

"So you've met each other?" said the Herbalist, giving the girl a small dry biscuit to eat with her hot drink. "He left the town early this morning. He had to return home. He's on a business mission from the east. He's young, but he's a good trader and already commands high respect. He knows six or seven languages and has travelled widely. He takes after his father."

"But he can't go! I have something for him," said Jade Fish, disappointed. "I wanted to ask him some questions. He might know what happened to Fan Lian."

"Fan Lian?" said the woman warily. "What do you want to know about her for? I know only that Zhou Ting's sister is almost certainly dead. The queen was a jealous, ruthless woman. She not only had no children herself, but her husband was supposedly attracted to her pretty young sister. When Fan Lian fell into disgrace, the king could no longer protect her. It was hushed up, though I'm certain it was the queen who gave orders for her death."

"But what was her disgrace?" asked Jade Fish.

"I don't know," replied the Herbalist. "Nobody really knew and nobody dared to utter her name again. Fan Lian disappeared and the queen seemed happier. The king looked as if he had been cast into the shadows."

2   Ling Hu entered the chamber. He told the girl how he had found her and carried her back. He said how worried they had all been.

"It was a cobra," Jade Fish told him. "A young snake, I think. I saw it clearly."

"I guessed as much," said the Herbalist. "An older one would almost certainly have killed you. As it was, I had a hard job keeping your breathing going. The poison affects your breathing. I used concoctions I prepared from a special bark and from various leaves. Speed is what counts. If Ling Hu had not applied that tight bandage and if he had not hurried here, my job might have been far harder, if not impossible."

"Thank you, Ling Hu!" said the girl humbly. "Thank you for saving my life. Might I beg another favour of you?"

Ling Hu bowed. The girl studied him more closely; he was strong and handsome for his years, very different from the young man who had been so proud and angry in the cave.

"Of course," he replied. "I should like you to think well of me."

"Would you ride to the eastern highway and see if you can see Bien Jin, the Emissary's son? He was working for someone from the east."

"But I have no idea what he looks like. There might be hundreds of travellers. He might be miles away by now," said Ling Hu looking a little disappointed by his task.

"Oh, *please!*" begged the girl with all the strength she could summon. "I have to give him something." Jade Fish gave a brief description of the boy she had met. She dropped her eyes and blushed as she spoke.

"I'm not sure if that's really why you want Ling Hu to fetch him here," laughed Nang Soo Chong.

Ling Hu hesitated a moment longer before he strode out of the room, unsmilingly and without a word.

"Is he angry?" asked Jade Fish, worried. "Have I done something wrong?"

"He's not angry," said the woman soothingly. "He's a good young man and he has gone to do the best he can. Of that I'm sure. I think he… likes and admires you. He told me about the events in the mountains and he's ashamed of his past behaviour."

3   Ling Hu galloped his horse to the main square where crowds were milling around, some trading and bartering, some loading waggons, and some busy packing or sorting goods for delivery. He searched this way and that, but failed to see any young man setting off.

Taking the eastern road he spurred his horse on and overtook bands of merchants. There were camels laden with dates and pomegranates, strings of donkeys staggering under packs of cloth, whiskered old traders, families moving their belongings, and there were children trying to sell food or drinks to the passers-by. But, although Ling Hu rode for nine miles and passed many travellers, he never crossed the handsome youth that Jade Fish had described.

Turning his horse who was tiring, he walked it back to the palace to report his lack of success.

"I'm sorry, Jade Fish," he said when he returned to the girl's bedside in the Herbalist's house. "I rode for nine miles and searched everywhere in the market square. He must have made good speed this morning for his return. There's no sign of him. He's gone."

"Oh, thank you, Ling Hu," said the girl, trying to hide her disappointment. "I don't know what I can do. That boy was my last hope."

"May I be able to help you instead?" said the young warrior meekly. "You can always rely on me for assistance."

"Oh, Ling Hu, I owe you everything in the world!" smiled the girl. "Of course I value your aid and your offer of help in the future. But I do so wish I could have talked to Bien Jin."

At that moment, who should walk in as if by magi,c but Bien Jin himself? He greeted Nang Soo Chong warmly, bowed to Ling Hu courteously and then addressed Jade Fish with a smile.

"I was delayed this morning by a meeting that went on far longer than I expected. Then, as I was setting out some people said a man from Nang Soo Chong's house had been looking for me urgently."

"That will have been Ling Hu," said Jade Fish, indicating the young man with a warm smile. "He was the one who found me and I owe him my life."

Bien Jin bowed a second time to the young man before continuing.

"Of course I changed my plans," he said earnestly, "and I came straight away when I realised you had been asking for me. I'm so pleased that you have recovered. I thought when we spoke that you were mending well. You must be a very strong girl and we all know how Nang Soo Chong's remedies are famed to work marvels."

The girl blushed for a second time that day and she lowered her eyes.

"Thank you, Bien Jin. I'm so grateful you returned. I... I have something to give you that belongs to you. It's important."

"But who are you?" asked the boy, sitting on her bed and staring into her shining eyes. "Have we met before?"

The girl shook her head, smiling.

"How have you got something that belongs to me? You're surely not one of those terrible robbers we've all heard about, are you?"

Jade Fish screwed up her face and tried to make it look fierce and evil while Bien Jin laughed delightedly.

Neither of them noticed, but at that precise moment Ling Hu slipped discreetly from the room. He didn't give the girl or boy a backward glance but his head was bowed and he had a dark scowl on his face.

4   "The Jade Lion!" cried Bien Jin, staring at the smooth white lion on a leather collar, which the girl had just given him. "My father told us once a story about three jade pieces. We never knew

if it was a true story, for he was a great storyteller when my brothers and I were growing up.

"He said that the king had once asked him to order a jade fish necklace for the queen's younger sister whom Zhou Hin liked very much. So my father went to the Royal Jade Carver and ordered a remarkable pendant of a most exquisite fish, a carp, made of green jade. It was so beautiful that my father immediately wanted to have a red jade piece carved for his own wife, my mother, in the shape of a tortoise, and a lion in white jade for his baby son. This was me.

"The king gave the jade fish pendant to the queen's sister on her birthday, and, according to my father, this was very badly received by the queen who became exceedingly jealous.

"Luckily, my father was able to give my mother the red jade tortoise, but before he could collect the white lion a terrible thing happened. The princess was found out to have committed an indiscretion, my father said, and the queen flew into a quite terrible rage."

"An indiscretion?" cried the girl, her hand flying up to her mouth, "But surely I am not the king's... daughter?"

"Why should you say that?" asked the boy.

As he spoke Jade Fish reached out to the bedside table and showed him the jade fish, which the Herbalist had removed when the girl's throat had been constricted by the poison of the cobra.

Bien Jin was amazed. In one hand he held up and stared at the necklace, comparing the craftsmanship of the fish with that of the carved lion, which he was held in his other hand.

"The king might well have committed ... an indiscretion with

Fan Lian and I might be his daughter," said Jade Fish wonderingly.

Bien Jin was amused and shook his head.

"No, you cannot be, for you have not heard the end of the story, which is not a happy one. My honourable father is dead now, as you must have been told, but he was renowned for his integrity and his absolute honesty. He only told us the ending of the story on his deathbed, two years ago, because he said he had been obliged to tell lies, something which went utterly against his character.

"The queen demanded first that the Jade Carver and his wife were to be killed. My father assured her on his honour that this had been done, but in fact he arranged for the Stone Cutter and his wife to steal away at night to another place, far away.

"Next, the queen told my father to have her sister followed, as she suspected her of having a lover and she was terrified it might be the king. So, my father, himself, followed Fan Lian. It was much too delicate an operation in which to involve junior counsellors."

Jade Fish's eyes were wide open with interest as she gazed up at the handsome boy.

"My father," Bien Jin continued, "followed the girl one day. She slipped away all alone on her beautiful white horse. She told nobody about this for it would have been unheard of for a young woman, particularly a princess, to be outside the palaces without an escort."

"Where did she go?" asked the girl.

"She went up into the hills. My father never found out whom she met for she noticed him and ordered him back. But she did meet someone, clearly, for later he learned that there was a baby child, a little girl."

"Me?" asked Jade Fish, unable to bear the suspense.

"Possibly," said the boy cautiously. "But, you see, the queen heard maids gossiping and she found out about the baby, and then things became very dark, indeed, for my poor father, even though he assured Zhou Ting the Queen that the baby was not the king's.

"The queen summoned my father to a secret meeting with Fan Lian and the king. She told her sister that she and the king had discovered her secret and that she would have to be sent away without her baby who would be given to another couple to adopt and bring up. She told her sister that it was because of the shame that Fan Lian might bring upon the Peacock Throne.

"Her sister, Princess Fan Lian, wept bitterly and begged and begged to be allowed to keep her baby. She said she would disappear and go far away if only she could keep her child. But she was told that it was impossible. The guards took Fan Lian away, screaming, and she was kept in a locked room for three days.

"After her sister had been dragged away, Zhou Ting then told my father that he *personally* had to strangle Fan Lian along with her chambermaid and close friend, Li Po. The queen ordered my father to do this in order to make sure that the story ended there."

"How terrible!" cried Jade Fish. "But what about the baby?"

"She ordered my father to kill the baby too. The child was not at the palace, but she was at a secret location that only my father knew about. The king, who was present, merely nodded to show that he agreed with his wife's decision."

"So your father... murdered Fan Lian?" asked the girl horrified.

"No, of course he didn't!" said Bien Jin shaking his head. "But he brought back the jade fish as proof that he had strangled the girl and thrown her body, and that of Li Po, in the river. The queen was delighted that her sister had been disposed of and she insisted that my father should keep the jewel as a reward for his loyalty.

"What haunted my father for the rest of his life was the fact that he lied. He had already hidden the truth about the Jade Cutter and his wife. Now, he solemnly swore, on his oath of allegiance and all that he held to be true, that he had personally killed Fan Lian, the mother, and her baby child. You have to understand that for my father, with his reputation for absolute honesty, this was a serious blow, even though he could have argued that he was doing it from the best motives."

"So, what really happened to them?" asked Jade Fish, on tenterhooks to know her history.

"My father personally guided Fan Lian and her servant friend to a town three days away in the east. They left on horseback at night under cover of darkness. From there he arranged for her to be accompanied by merchant friends of his to an important diplomat living in the far east; who would give her protection and who could be relied upon to be very discreet.

"So she is alive?"

"She might be. She was alive just before my father's death, for I saw him writing to her," said Bien Jin.

"And the baby? Why couldn't Fan Lian take the baby with her? What happened to the little girl?"

"Ah, now that's more uncertain," said the boy. "My father, of course, didn't want the poor little baby killed and he was quite ready to have the child sent to Fan Lian secretly later on. But the queen wanted proof that Fan Lian had not hidden the child before she was killed. She wished to see Fan Lian's jade fish and she wanted to see the baby before it was killed."

"How awful! What a horrible woman!" cried Jade Fish.

"My father thinks that she was not only exceedingly jealous of her sister, who was attractive, intelligent and sociable, but she also feared that Fan Lian's children would inherit the Throne."

"But Zhou Ting had no children of her own," protested the girl.

"Precisely - that must have made it even worse in her mind."

"So, what did your father do with the baby?" asked Jade Fish.

"He told us, just before he died, that a week after Fan Lian had gone, he took the baby to show the queen and then put it in a cradle for the night. It was far too late and much too risky to think of sending the baby east in search of its mother.

"In the morning, he gave the baby to an elderly gardener, whom he trusted absolutely, and he told this man to find a couple somewhere far away, who could look after the baby temporarily, until such time as it was safe to take her to her real mother, Fan Lian. He gave the gardener a bag of gold, which could be used by the couple to look after the child as it grew up. But nobody, absolutely no one, was to know anything about the child's origins.

"The queen summoned him so she could gloat over her management of the whole affair. My father told the queen that the baby was dead and that he had thrown the little girl into the river."

"So your father gave the baby to the Gardener?" whispered the girl in amazement. "But then, who was this baby's father? And why wasn't the baby later reunited with her mother?"

Bien Jin had no idea.

5   The next morning the girl seemed strong enough to leave the Herbalist's house. Bien Jin accompanied her back to the palaces his father had spoken about so much. His son had seen them on his various business missions but he had never actually visited them.

"Why is your family living in the east?" asked Jade Fish as they walked back past the ornamental lake.

"All the heart went out of my father after these events," replied Bien Jin. "I'm sure that they were partly responsible for his falling sick in the Lands of Qin. My father had been strong and healthy all his life. But after he died, my mother wished to move as far away from this kingdom as possible."

The boy had stayed last night again at the Herbalist's house, but he was keen to return home quickly, as he was on an important business mission. He was, however, most interested in finding out who Jade Fish was, almost as interested as the girl was herself.

They found the Gardener busy as usual. This time he was at the back of the palaces, where it was wild. He was hacking away at the undergrowth and chopping down vegetation. Jade Fish was concerned, for it was very hard work, almost impossible for one man on his own. It would have needed several teams of gardeners to begin to make any headway at all on the thick jungle where Jade Fish had come so close to losing her life.

"This terrible wilderness!" he exclaimed as they drew near. "It's more than I can cope with, but somebody has to try. I heard it nearly cost a young girl her life the other day! It's my responsibility to oversee these gardens. What if they were allowed to become totally wild?"

Jade Fish, said to the man, "This is Bien Jin, the Emissary's son." The man dropped his machete in amazement and stared at the handsome young man standing before him. He didn't say a word.

"My father spoke of you," said Bien Jin, smiling in a friendly manner at the elderly man. "He told me a story about a little baby."

The old Gardener's eyes widened in horror and he turned to stare at Jade Fish.

The girl pointed to the jade fish around her throat.

"You know about this?" she asked sternly. "Why did you say nothing when we arrived? You must have seen it."

"I... I was... sworn to absolute secrecy by that boy's father, the Emissary," mumbled the old man in broken tones. "I was also scared because of what I had done. Bien Manchu, the Emissary told me to make sure that I found the baby a home, people who would look after her."

"Why didn't you do that?" demanded the girl. "I was left out on the mountainside to perish."

"I tried to find a family. The baby girl was wrapped in a beautiful royal shawl and she had a fine necklace, but nobody wanted to adopt a girl. Even for gold. Your father had given me gold to help persuade people to adopt the child. 'A boy?' they all said. 'Perhaps. But a girl? And a girl with royal connections. Never!'

I told them it would only be for a few years, but in all my travels I found nobody prepared to adopt the little baby girl.

"It was up in the mountains near a pass with a steep gorge when I finally found an elderly merchant. I was getting desperate by then. I showed him the gold and his eyes lit up. 'I'll take her and look after her exceedingly well,' he promised. I could see that he was not totally trustworthy, but I didn't know what else to do. And he was a merchant, at least.

"I should never have left that child!" he muttered, wiping away a tear.

"I was that baby!" stated the girl indignantly. "You must have guessed."

"You? Yes, you were that baby. Everything is clearer now," muttered the old man, ashamed. "I think that I knew it when I first saw you. I was hoping that it was a different jade fish or else that you had acquired it somehow. I saw it on your neck the first day, but I was too frightened by what I'd done. I've been living with this secret for too long. We never found the merchant again and so the Emissary and I just hoped that he would have looked after the child."

"Who, then, is my father?" demanded Jade Fish.

6   A lone mynah bird screeched its distress about something from high in the trees. The sun beat down upon the thickets and dense undergrowth. Mayflies hovered in the still afternoon and two stray monkeys came swinging through the overarching branches, as if to witness the scene. But they left chattering angrily when they saw there was no chance of being fed.

"Your father swore me to secrecy, of course," said the Gardener, turning to the son of the Emissary. "I was the only person apart from him and Fan Lian herself to know the identity of her lover."

"But who? Who was her lover if not the king? Who was the father of the baby girl, of me?" asked the girl insistently.

"Why, the Robber Baron, of course!" said the old Gardener. "Your father is Yuan Song."

"Yuan... Song, the Robber!" gasped the girl, almost speechless with surprise. "How could...? He's my father? But he's still here! I must go and find..."

It was then that she fainted from the shock. Bien Jin rushed to catch her and, with the Gardener helping as best he could, the boy carried her to sit by a fallen tree trunk to recover.

The Gardener hobbled off to fetch some water from one of the drinking fountains in the royal gardens and he returned a few minutes later with a man on horseback.

It was Yuan Song. The Gardener, in terror, had said nothing about the conversations that had taken place. He had merely told the Robber Baron that Jade Fish had returned but had fainted.

Yuan Song had already spoken with Ling Hu, so he knew that the Emissary's son was with her. He leapt down from his horse and strode over with a flask of water to see if the girl was better.

She rose unsteadily to her feet as he approached.

"Are you all right, Jade Fish?" he asked. "The Gardener said you had fainted. We have water for you. A cobra bite is serious. I don't think you should be walking too far until you have properly recovered."

"I'm all right," answered the girl shakily, sipping at the flask. "It was not the cobra bite that caused me to faint. It was the news of who I am... I'm perfectly well now.

"Thank you for the water, *Father!*"

7   "What did you call me?" demanded Yuan Song, astonished. "Did you say 'Father'?"

"I remember you told us that you had a wife once and a baby girl," said Jade Fish unsteadily. "What do you recall of them?"

Yuan Song looked at her closely and uncertainly.

"My wife was very beautiful. She said her name was Liu Bao. She came from a poor family who lived in the east. I met her quite by chance when she was out riding alone. She said she had stolen the horse from a rich palace and I laughed and told her that if she liked, I would return with her and steal anything she wanted.

"She found that funny and laughed with me, but she said that it was out of the question. She wore good clothes and looked extremely elegant, but whenever I asked, she would reply that she knew how to steal better than I did. She would say, 'In clothes I am rich, but in fortune I'm very poor!'"

Jade Fish could not help laughing.

"Yuan Song, Father, that woman was the younger sister of the queen, Zhou Ting! Her name is Fan Lian. I believe that I'm her daughter and yours too."

"I can't believe that!" exclaimed the Robber Baron, utterly amazed. "You? You are the baby we had? She saw me at regular intervals for nearly a year. She left our child for me to look after. I had a servant woman who cared for the baby when Liu Bao was not there. We called the little girl Yuan Niou-niou.

"But one day, she and the child suddenly disappeared. I returned to find them both gone. I thought she couldn't accept my way of life, for she had often shown me that really she disapproved of my activities. I was heartbroken, for there was no goodbye nor explanation. And I'd grown to love that little baby."

The hardened bandit, now a bandit no longer, surreptitiously wiped away a tear from the corner of his eye with the back of his hairy hand.

Bien Jin then spoke up.

"My father, sir, saved the king's sister-in-law, the woman you knew as Liu Bao. He saved her from being murdered and he decided to save her child as well. He risked his life to do so, as you have no idea how dangerous things were in the palaces at that time. My father ordered this man," he indicated the old Gardener, who was helping Jade Fish to drink some more water, "to find foster parents for your baby. He tried to find a couple who could adopt her far from the queen and king who wanted her killed. He found no one except an unreliable merchant who took the gold but left the baby on the roadside. Luckily, a shepherd couple discovered her on the mountainside. It sounds incredible, but, believe me, sir, this really is your daughter."

"Yuan Niou-niou!" said Jade Fish. "Was that my name? Father, I am so happy to have found you at last. There is a chance that my mother, too, is still alive. The Emissary was in contact with her two years ago before he died. She probably now lives in the east if all is still well."

"Just as I thought, and as, indeed, she gave me hints," murmured Yuan Song, still dazed by the news that Jade Fish was his very own daughter. "We were registered as man and wife, but in secret. She told me she was too poor in fortune to have a proper wedding and that she came from a terrible family, to whom I should be ashamed to be related."

He laughed at the thought. Then he held open his arms and clasped the girl, who had rushed over finally to hug him. The hug lasted for a few minutes and not a word was said by either.

Then Yuan Song laughed again as he had another thought.

"Jade Fish, Yuan Niou-niou, Daughter! There is nobody else left in the lineage of Zhou Ting. You and your mother must be the heirs to the Peacock Throne. You could be its new princess!"

So saying, the smile left his face and he put both his hands together. Then he fell on his knees.

At almost the same moment, Bien Jin and the Gardener also went down on their knees and placed their hands together with their fingers also pointing towards the heavens.

Jade Fish took a deep breath. This time she didn't faint.

8   All at once events began to unfold with almost frightening speed.

News, first of all, spread about the town, like one of those forest fires which suddenly blaze out among the dry bushes and whose fierce flames are fanned steadily by the winds of chance. Yet, the real power of such fires is the way that they creep, steadily and speedily, under the ground, deep beneath the dry vegetation. They cannot be easily put out and they are impelled by all that simmering energy, which from time to time breaks out with orange tongues, excitedly and exactingly, right up to the tops of the trees.

So it was with the rumours that a rightful claimant to the throne had been almost magically discovered. All round the town you could see people huddling in groups and running from one gathering to another.

"Is it true that a young princess has really been discovered and she is actually next in line to the Peacock Throne?"

"I don't know for sure, but what have you heard? I believe it is a young kitchen servant!"

"No! How can that be? A princess cannot be a kitchen servant and neither can a kitchen girl be a princess! That's unheard of!"

Jade Fish called a meeting the following day in the Hall of the Peacock Throne. It was strange how suddenly she had acquired an authority which nobody had suspected her of having before. Clapping her hands together she directed one of the younger servant boys to fetch Yuan Song and his band of reformed robbers. She summoned also the Nurse, Mu Ju, Nang Soo Chong the Herbalist, Bien Jin the Emissary's son, the Gardener and the Cook to attend a special meeting.

"I've called you here," she announced in a firm, clear voice, "because it seems that I might be the next in line to the throne. If that is so, it is a responsibility which I must consider very carefully. But, first I must ask you, Yuan Song, if I really am your daughter. Is there any documentary proof of your marriage?"

Yuan Song had lost much of his composure and much, too, of his former bluster.

"Yes, your Highness," he muttered. "Your mother and I were married far away. But I had no idea that she was of royal lineage. She told me she was poor."

"Father, that wasn't my question," said Jade Fish gently but firmly. "Was it properly witnessed and sealed?"

"Certainly, my daughter," he said meekly. "It was the Magistrate who married us."

"The Magistrate?" gasped the girl. "Not the Magistrate of the Border Town?"

The man nodded.

"Then I shall have to summon him here too," said the girl, "and with the necessary documents to prove my title. Ling Hu, stand forth, please!"

Ling Hu stepped forward but he dropped his eyes and couldn't look at Jade Fish directly.

"What does your Royal Highness request?" he said somewhat guardedly. "Ask and it shall be done."

"Sir, I know we can count on you absolutely, for you saved my life and you shall not find me ungrateful," said the girl. "I wish you to take three men with you. I've heard in the town that there's a quicker road to the Border Town than by taking the route we came on through the mountains. Is this true?"

"Yes, your Majesty," said Yuan Song, almost forgetting that he was addressing his young daughter. "There is indeed a quicker road that skirts the mountains. Don't you wish me to go with Ling Hu?"

"No, Father," said Jade Fish. "I need you to be head of our security force here. Bien Jin, I'm creating you our Emissary, if you agree to serve us in that capacity."

The boy smiled and bowed.

"Nothing would please me more," he said. "I need, however, to finish my business mission first."

"I agree. Nang Soo Chong," said the girl, turning to the Herbalist. "I should like you to be on our staff as Counsellor. I have seen enough to know that you are wise and capable."

The woman bowed and so did the Gardener and the Cook, when Jade Fish appointed them Heads of the Household and asked them to organise the servants and appoint any missing officials who might be needed.

"I have no funds as yet to pay your wages," said Jade Fish apologetically, "but once the government is properly established with an appropriate security force to keep law and order, correct taxes will then be raised to ensure that the country is rightfully and fairly managed. It's possible that I may be confirmed as your ruler eventually, but it's by no means clear, for legal documents proving entitlement must be sought and my mother may well wish to rule, as she has every right to do. If, however, the choice falls on me, I would wish to be a ruler who consults, and is consulted by, her people. I wish that to be known from the outset."

The girl bowed and indicated to the group before her that the audience was now over. She then motioned to Bien Jin that she wished to speak with him.

"Bien Jin," she said, "your first mission when you finish your business dealing is to seek Fan Lian, my mother, and request her attendance here. If she really is my mother, I have to talk with her and know more about her. If she is the rightful heir to the Throne, then she must be invested as Queen."

Bien Jin bowed low, but he gave the girl a warm smile as he did so.

"Where did you learn to speak like *that*?" he whispered.

The girl coloured, but then she smiled back.

"I learned a lot at the back of the Magistrate's court!" she whispered back to him.

9   "Ling Hu," said Jade Fish in the courtyard after her audience. They were on their own and he was preparing to ride out on horseback with three of his fellows and make his way to the Border Town. "Listen carefully to my instructions."

"Yes, your Majesty," answered Ling Hu. He now raised his eyes and looked at Jade Fish. One could tell that he admired the girl and was very taken by her, more so than he might ever have imagined from their first meeting.

"I want you and your three guards," directed Jade Fish, "to require the Magistrate of the Border Town, on my strictest orders, to attend me here, bearing with him the document of my parents' marriage registration. I particularly wish his wife to accompany him to the meeting. If they do not come willingly, then you are to enforce this order. It must be done immediately."

"I shall do this," said Ling Hu, bowing low. "Thank you, your Majesty, for putting your trust in my abilities. I wish to serve you as faithfully and honourably as heaven may see fit."

"I am extremely grateful to you, Ling Hu," said the girl, "but listen further, as I have one more instruction."

Ling Hu paused, with his foot already up in the stirrup, ready to mount his horse. In the background were his fellow bandits, already in their saddles and circling about the yard, impatient to be off.

"You are to arrest Yin Hsi and Lao Tzu," said Jade Fish calmly, "and I wish you to bring them here with the Magistrate and his wife as quickly as possible. If you ride fast you will be at the Border Town before Lao Tzu can pass through to the lands of Qin. What he is aiming to do is illegal, of course, and he must be brought here, with his scrolls, to defend his actions. The Gatekeeper must accompany him. They are breaking the law.

"Arrest them?" gasped Ling Hu. "Are you mad? They are your friends!"

"You heard my orders, Ling Hu," said the girl, her face set and her voice uncharacteristically cold and hard. "I'm certainly not mad. I wish them all to be brought here to me. In chains, if necessary!"

The softest substance in the universe, water,
Overwhelms the hardest: rock.
That which has no form can invade
Even where there is no space..
Hence, I know the value of inaction.
Teaching without words and acting without doing anything
Is something understood by very few.

(**Tao Tê Ching** - The Classic of the Way and Its Virtue - XLIII)

PART NINE

Others may be radiant, as if at a feast,
As if it were springtime and they were climbing a tower,
I alone remain quiet, forlorn, like one uncertain,
Like a baby yet to smile.
Lonely and sad, I seem to have no home.
Others may have plenty; I, alone, appear hollow and empty.
I seem stupid and ignorant.
Others may be bright; I, alone, seem dull.
Others may be intelligent; I, alone seem confused,
As lonely as an ocean wave and drifting with the wind.
Others may have goals; I, alone seem awkward and clumsy.
I, alone, seem to differ from all others.
But what I most prize is feeding
From the milk of eternal Nature, our mother.
Not understanding the eternal we act blindly
And we court catastrophe.

(**Tao Tê Ching** - The Classic of the Way and Its Virtue - XX)

I   At this dramatic point in our story we must pause to draw breath. It took nine long days before Bien Jin returned from his journey to fetch Fan Lian, and those nine days during his absence were packed with business and events.

Very soon, as the news spread to the surrounding regions, courtiers from the former monarchy under Zhou Ting began to arrive in the town. Fine gentlemen and even finer ladies in colourful silks and elaborate hair styles let it be known that they were willing to serve as palace courtiers and functionaries once again, this time in the service of Zhou Ting's sister.

Jade Fish, accompanied by her Head of Security, her father Yuan Song, personally interviewed and rejected many, though it was expedient to re-engage some of the officials who had worked there previously. Jade Fish made it clear, however, when these people were sworn in, how different the organisation of the court was to be in future. There would be more informality and more attention paid to effective administration and welfare. There would also be much more accountability and far more insistence on compassion and benevolence than before.

Yuan Song recruited former palace guards, whom he began to retrain as a proper and effective security force. As he said, without a trace of irony apparently:

"This country is beset with robbers and bandits; I should know, for I was one of them once. The land needs protection against marauders and thieves, but without violence, of course. Society must protect the weakest against the strongest and the most powerful."

Very soon the palaces were functioning smoothly: diplomats were received or dispatched with orders, business people were interviewed, and trustworthy judges appointed. Teachers were trained and soup-kitchens opened, where the poorest would find food. Parades, too, were held, where Jade Fish was seen in public and where she or her spokesman, a young functionary from the east, carefully explained to people the new aims of Jade Fish's administration.

A messenger was sent to Chan Shui the Wise Woman with an invitation to return to the court as the Royal Oracle. The messenger later returned saying that Chan Shui was most honoured and would return if the *I Ching* favoured such a move.

"In the meantime," announced the messenger, "Chan Shui has sent back this packhorse with her daughter's clothes."

As promised, Jade Fish wore the beautiful silk suits of the Wise Woman's daughter, for, in fact, she had very little else to wear until the Court Tailors were set to work once more.

On the ninth day, Bien Jin reappeared with a mysterious woman who was veiled and dressed very simply in a dark woollen cloak and shawl. They arrived late in the evening and the woman met with nobody, retiring to her bedchamber straight away.

In the morning Fan Lian asked to be presented to her daughter.

2   Jade Fish found her mother standing on the veranda overlooking the sun-filled lake and gardens. She had been speaking with her old Nurse Mu Ju, but she was now alone, staring out at the peaceful view.

"So," her mother said, turning to look at the girl, "I'm told that you are my daughter!"

Tears welled up in the woman's lovely almond-shaped eyes of a deep jade green, as she drew back her veil and revealed her beautiful face.

"Yes!" she whispered. "There can be no doubt, even if I had not seen my green jade fish necklace again. You are quite how I was once. I see a lot of myself in you."

"Can you *really* be my mother?" asked Jade Fish shyly. The woman before her was elegant and beautiful with a warm smile and a low, gentle voice.

The woman nodded, unable to speak for a moment. Then she reached to hold the girl in her arms and her tears fell freely. Jade Fish found herself sobbing too, crying with the relief that so many years of pain and unhappiness now lay in the dusty past. She had both her parents at last. It was like a dam breaking. The wall of fortitude she had built up over such a long time gave way finally, and the years of sorrow trickled in small streams down her cheeks.

"You cannot know, my child, how much I have missed you," said Fan Lian at last, wiping her own eyes and her daughter's. "You should know that I never, never wanted to give you up. But I was completely powerless. The Emissary, Bien Manchu, told me he would try to send you back to me, but that I would have to wait and be patient.

"My sister Zhou Ting was so jealous and so utterly determined that the throne should not pass to me or my children.

Anyone who tried to help me risked immediate death.

"It was only thanks to the Emissary that I escaped with my friend, Li Po. Li Po is the grand-daughter of my dear nurse, Mu Ju. Her mother died in childbirth and her grandmother brought her up as her own daughter. I have just been telling Mu Ju about her and why Li Po had been unable to contact her before now.

"We escaped secretly to the east, knowing that if we were discovered we would certainly be killed, as would the Emissary, who had done so much to protect both us and the Jade Cutter. However, I nearly didn't go because I was so heartbroken, thinking that my baby daughter was already dead. I just wanted to drown myself in the river. Li Po cared for me and took charge of me and the Emissary later sent us word that the baby had been temporarily adopted. Then months later he sent me a terrible letter saying that there had been an accident and that you had died. I was so wretched after that. Luckily I had Li Po to help me bear my loss."

"All my life, I hoped and hoped that my parents were still living," sobbed Jade Fish through her own tears. "I never had any idea that I was high-born. Not until the shepherds showed me the silk shawl recently, and then I began to wonder."

They talked and talked thus for many hours. Jade Fish had so much to relate and she had so many questions to ask her mother. In response Fan Lian was very curious about Yuan Song and about how he had recently renounced his bad past.

"But, Mother," said the girl, "do you not now wish to rule as the rightful queen? These palaces are now yours. You could rule the state and repair all the harms that have happened. Wouldn't you like to do that and live here once more?"

"No," said Fan Lian firmly. "The Emissary's son spoke a lot about you on the journey here. He is very taken with you and thinks that you might make an excellent ruler. I have discovered a new life for myself in the east. I work quietly and happily as a teacher. I live with Li Po, who is my best friend. We both built and opened our school and we teach girls and boys together. The children live with us and learn from us."

"Mu Ju must have been thrilled to hear that her grand-daughter was living. Will Li Po not visit her grandmother now?" asked Jade Fish.

Fan Lian nodded.

"We ran away together. I could not have survived had it not been for Li Po, who assisted in our escape and protected me on the road. She dressed as a young man so we should have fewer problems on our travels."

At this moment, a servant approached and, bowing, asked whether Fan Lian would give an audience to Yuan Song, the Head of the Palace Guards. Fan Lian assented and Yuan Song entered the chamber. The two faced each other and bowed deeply.

"So, you really are Fan Lian," he said softly after a long pause, when they had both studied each other carefully. "You are still as beautiful as when I first met you, though your name has changed! I knew you as Liu Bao."

The woman shook her head, smiling.

"You said you weren't rich, then," continued Yuan Song. "I only found out recently who you really were."

"I'm still not rich,"laughed Fan Lian, "though I am not as poor as I was in those days. And look at our daughter! Is she not wealth enough? Look what a lovely girl we have produced, you and I."

"Have you heard of what has become of me?" asked Yuan Song. "I met Lao Tzu and I've reformed. My men and I are palace security guards now."

"So I've heard," said Fan Lian, smiling at his seriousness. "I, too, am very interested in the teachings of Lao Tzu. They are also in part the reason why I don't wish to rule."

"Ah," said Yuan Song thoughtfully. "I think I can understand that. But what's your other reason for not wishing to become queen, if I might ask?"

"Yuan Song, the Robber Baron, who stole my heart once," said Fan Lian with a little laugh, "please try to understand me. Once I was your wife, briefly, but bad people and bad events forced us apart and our destinies took different paths. I am now living with my best friends in the east and we have a life together as teachers and companions. You must not think that I can retrace my footsteps. You and I have a daughter and a history, but we will never be husband and wife again. I hope, however, that we can continue to meet as good friends."

"That's all right," answered Yuan Song after another long pause, while he looked deeply into the eyes of his former wife. "I do understand you, I think. I like the company of my men and I have no real wish to live a domestic life, settled at home with a wife and family. I love my work and I'm happy to serve my state, our kingdom, and help improve the lives of our people. Much has changed for me.

"Our lives, as you say, have moved on. The Wise Woman showed us, when she read our fortunes in the *I Ching*, that all human life is governed by change. Change, she said, is not to be feared but should instead be welcomed, for our lives will always be subject to growth and the hazards of chance."

Jade Fish looked from one to another. Her life, too, was shifting rapidly. Wasn't this 'Return' what the *I Ching* had predicted: an opportunity? She had found her parents and they seemed to like and respect each other, but it was still not quite the happy ending she had sometimes dreamed about.

"Will I still see you?" she asked her mother anxiously. "I have only just found you. I don't want to lose you straight away."

"Oh, my dearest child!" cried her mother, taking the girl in her arms again. "We will see each other often. You will visit us very soon, I hope, and we shall come here as often as we can. And when, in the future, I become a grandmother, I shall return even more. You will find it hard to get rid of me."

"Grandmother!" exclaimed the girl. "What can possibly have given you the thought of grandchildren already? I am only thirteen!"

"Not now, my dear," said the woman hastily. "I merely meant in the future, one day, perhaps."

3   Bien Jin, as if on cue, entered the room, ushered in by the same servant who had just shown out Yuan Song.

"I hope I'm not intruding, your Highnesses," he said a little uncertainly to Jade Fish. "I am needed at home and I wished to know, Fan Lian, if you wanted me to escort you back to the east, or if you will stay here as ruler."

"I shall return with this very attractive young man!" declared Fan Lian, her eyes dancing with amusement, for she evidently liked the Emissary's son, about whom, of course, she had already heard.

"Jade Fish, or Yu Yù," she continued, "will become the rightful ruler when she comes of age. Until then, I should like her to rule with the help of her father, Yuan Song, if he is willing to act as Regent and First Counsellor. I shall return here for the Investiture and for the Coronation at a later date. But my schoolchildren right now are waiting for me and I shall gladly return home with you as my escort."

Jade Fish looked sad.

"Must you go already?" she asked her mother and Bien Jin. "I need both of you. I have so little experience and I was hoping you might stay here to help."

"Your Highness," replied Bien Jin, smiling at the girl, "I'm not going away for long, I assure you. I wish to help you and serve you. If I may, I'll bring my mother back with her household. She's always dreamed of returning here."

"Oh, Bien Jin!" cried the girl. "What you say makes me much happier. I'll miss you.... or rather, I should say, we will miss you!

Please hurry back and do take great care to avoid all dangers on your journey!"

At this, they all laughed, as did Jade Fish, who was immediately covered in confusion and turned as red as the palace roof tiles. Fan Lian hugged her newly found daughter and they once again promised each other to be together very soon.

Fan Lian and Bien Jin departed the following morning, and they were seen off in style. All the palace staff lined up along the driveway leading from the palace. Musicians played, drummers drummed and dancers, dressed as lions and dragons in red and green, cavorted in front of the carriage. Yuan Song and his Palace Guards rode with the carriage as far as the outer limits of the town.

More meetings were held later on with important counsellors, merchants and diplomats. Jade Fish was very interested in all state matters and often interrupted the meetings to ask questions. If she received a muddled or unreasonable response, then her reaction was always to say,

"We shall proceed no further in this matter until it is explained and dealt with more intelligently or more humanely."

The girl's sympathies always lay with the poorer, more vulnerable people.

"But, your Highness," one or two of the older counsellors might protest. "I don't think you understand the situation properly. It has always been done in this way."

"Well, then, please explain exactly why it was done that way," the girl would say adamantly. "If it's unreasonable, or just plain wrong, then we will simply have to change the way it's done."

4   Three days after Bien Jin and Fan Lian departed, a small party of travellers entered the town and made their way to the palace late in the evening. Four armed horsemen escorted a carriage, which contained the Magistrate and his Wife and two elderly men. One was old and enormous with huge ears; the other was tall and dressed in the uniform of a Palace Guard, though the colour of his green leather armour showed that he was from the Border Town. Some of the townspeople recognized them as the men who had been there a few days previously. They wondered why they had returned and where the handsome black water buffalo was.

Ling Hu had brought back Lao Tzu and Yin Hsi, not in chains, but under compulsion nevertheless. He had arrested them just as the Gatekeeper was on the point of opening the Gates at night to let Lao Tzu depart to the west. The Master had been about to start his final journey towards the forbidden lands of the Qin, but without his scrolls, which he had left with Yin Hsi. Shuïniù, the Water Buffalo, had been with Lao Tzu when the arrests were made and so was presently being looked after by Yin Nuan, the Gatekeeper's wife.

The new guests were made welcome, though Jade Fish herself did not come to greet them. She sent a message that she was busy with meetings, but that she would see them first thing on the following day.

Lao Tzu's great shoulders shook with laughter when he heard this.

"Ah, the burdens of government!" he chuckled, wiping his eyes. "There won't be many trout caught by our young ruler nowadays!"

The Magistrate said nothing but stared around at the beautiful interiors of the huge palace. His wife looked at the old man in disgust. They had certainly not enjoyed their enforced journey to the Palaces of the Peacock Throne in the company of an elderly palace guard, whom they knew to be the Town Gatekeeper, and the enormous old man who had apparently adopted the clumsy kitchen girl they had once employed in the kitchens.

"Good riddance to her!" thought the Magistrate's Wife! "And the huge old fellow with the big ears had taken up most of the space in the carriage. Intolerable it had been!"

She and her husband had been politely requested to attend the Court of the Peacock Throne on a matter of legality. This amounted to an absolute summons. They still had no idea who the new ruler was nor who had summoned them. Because neither of them had asked any questions or shown any curiosity about anything on their nine-day journey together, Lao Tzu and Yin Hsi had not felt it worth enlightening them. The couple had been most unfriendly and had merely tried to impress the two men with their importance and wealth.

Their efforts so far had been in vain.

5   Early the following morning, Lao Tzu was performing his morning exercises before the ornamental lake. It was a pearly-grey dawn with a hint of apricot above the town roofs on the far side of the shore, where the sun would rise in an hour's time. His

hands calmly and serenely described circles, where all was steady movement and slow transition, from pushing to withdrawing, from stepping to standing, from raising to lowering. Everything was changing in movement and nothing paused and nothing was strained. It was all so easy, so graceful and balanced.

Just as before, after a short while he became aware of the young girl behind him, practising the same movements in time with his. Delicately and lightly she kicked and Parted the Wild Horse's Mane (or *Yeh Ma Fen Tsung*). She was the Snake who Creeps down to the River to Drink (or *She Shen Hsia Shih*), and she was equally the Stork who Cools its Wings (or *Pai Hao Liang Ch'ih*). Just like her Master.

After the Grand Terminus (or *He T'ai Chi*) at the end, there was a pause as the Master listened to the real birds around him. They sang as if there were no tomorrow. Their whistles and calls, he knew, were to attract some and to dissuade others. Their chatter filled the trees. Finally, he turned around, but he knew, even as he did so, what he would find: an absence.

For the young girl had mysteriously vanished.

6   The guests congregated in a small ante-room to one side of the main assembly hall with the throne in the centre. They were at last shown in by Yuan Song to be seated in front of the empty throne.

"Please rise and make obeisance for her Royal Highness, the Princess Yu Yù!" commanded Yuan Song.

The company did as requested and, as they bowed low, the new ruler entered and took her seat on the Peacock Throne whose arms and back were brilliantly decked out with freshly painted peacock feathers of jade green with hundreds of shimmering blue eyes.

"Please be seated!" said a youthful voice.

As they sat back and looked up, the Magistrate's wife almost fell off her seat in her surprise at what she saw. A girl was sitting before them in a long silk dress of dark green, the colour of rich green jade, one of the dresses given to her by the Wise Woman. Her Royal Highness was none other than the wretched Kitchen Girl. *That* Kitchen Girl!

"Thank you for answering my request for an audience," said the new ruler of the Peacock Throne diplomatically, though, in truth, the visitors had been given no option by Ling Hu but to obey.

"I have summoned you," she said a little haughtily to the Magistrate, "to ensure the legality of my claim to the throne."

"Hah!" the wife of the Magistrate couldn't help uttering in her astonishment, not to mention anger. After a nine-day journey to be received by their common Kitchen Girl, and all dressed up in such silken finery! What was the world coming to?

"Aren't you that girl I used to see sometimes at the back of my court?" asked the Magistrate, staring hard at the young girl whom he barely recognised as their Kitchen Girl. Admittedly, he had scarcely ever visited his own kitchens.

"Oh!" exclaimed his wife, highly affronted. "So *that's* what she used to get up to when our backs were turned, is it?"

"I am the same girl, though somewhat changed. Never mind that now, sir," said the girl, addressing the Magistrate. "Do you recognize this man?" she asked, pointing at her father, Yuan Song.

The Magistrate looked in surprise again at the man, who was dressed in a superb uniform of dark red leather, with red woollen leggings and a red leather helmet. He was a handsome warrior of a man, with his tanned, grizzled face, bushy eyebrows and his thick grizzly locks and moustaches. His body was fit and rugged; he carried himself well. Yuan Song smiled amicably at the Magistrate from his place behind the Throne.

"I cannot say for sure," spluttered the Magistrate, feeling his wife's elbow digging him in the ribs. "I see so many plaintiffs from one year to the next."

"This man is no plaintiff," said the girl sharply. "This is my father and you have brought with you, I believe, the document where he registered with you the birth of his and Fan Lian's child?"

This was true. Ling Hu had ordered the Magistrate to bring the copy of the registration certificate for the child born to Yuan Song and the woman known as Fan Lian, or Liu Bao. Ling Hu now unrolled the scroll made of thin slats of bamboo woven together vertically on a grey silk screen.

"This is your mark on the document, is it not?" asked Jade Fish. The Magistrate nodded. His wife looked on, furious.

"Could you please answer, yes or no, before these witnesses?" asked Jade Fish, clearly remembering the style of questioning from the courtroom where, she said, she had been so intrigued by all the legal procedures.

"Yes," muttered the man. "The woman called herself Liu Bao, but she could write properly and she wrote the characters for Fan Lian. She also *wrote* the name for her husband. Here is the legal document."

He held up the scroll and pointed out the characters.

"And the child, a baby girl they called Yuan Niou-niou, was registered officially by you?" the girl continued.

"That appears to be the case," admitted the Magistrate, seeking to retain a little authority in this humiliating situation.

"Since I was that baby, who was then taken by the Gardener up to the Steep Gorges Rocks where I was luckily found by shepherds, that makes me, Yu Yù or Jade Fish, the legitimate daughter of Fan Lian, the sister of Zhou Ting," stated the girl. "I am therefore a member of the Zhou dynasty, and I am, as far as I know, the sole heir to this, the Peacock Throne if my mother declines to rule. And it so happens that my mother, Fan Lian, has announced that she wishes me to rule. So, whether I like it or not, I have to obey her."

The hand of the Magistrate's Wife sudenly flew to her mouth and she gasped with sudden dread.

"Oh, your Highness!" she managed to splutter. "Please look favourably on us. We were not to know who you were. We always tried to care for you!"

Jade Fish glanced at the Master, who was grinning from one big ear to the other big ear.

"You have no need to fear, Ning Mei," she said, gripping the massive arms of the Peacock Throne. "I am not vindictive, unlike some people. Perhaps in future, you might remember this: everybody has a right to kindness, courtesy and gentleness, children particularly. That you are the wife of the Magistrate does not make you a better or worthier person than anybody else. With privileges, you should know, come responsibilities. This is what I am finding out now.

"I wish you both well, however, and I hope you can be more charitable in future. You may depart."

The girl watched as the couple bowed to her and left the chamber without another word, either to her or to each other, and without even a backward glance.

She shook her head as if clearing her mind of bad memories, but she also allowed herself a little smile.

7   "Hah – herrmm!"

Lao Tzu gave a gentle cough, which resonated around the hall like the waves of a mighty sea pounding upon a rocky shore.

"Very impressive, my little Jade Fish!" he murmured, smiling at her. "But how much gentleness and courtesy have you shown Yin Hsi and myself, arresting us and ordering us here under an armed guard?"

There was a long pause.

"And in the pleasant company of the Magistrate and his charming wife."

"But what you were proposing, sir, was entirely illegal..." said the girl in a small voice. You could have heard a pin drop in the palace hall.

"Hah!" snorted the enormous old man. "You talk to me of legality, my dear? Is it of any consequence to anyone, where I choose to wander to end my life? This world is already too full of boundaries and *legalities*!"

There was a long silence, during which the young princess held his ironic gaze, before at last she dropped her eyes and furtively wiped some moisture from one of them.

Lao Tzu gave a great chuckle that rumbled cheerfully, somewhat like a heavy cart full of sweet and golden hay, creaking along a rough farm track up in the hills.

"Oh, I'm sorry, Master!" said Jade Fish, her head bowed, stricken with remorse. "I decided that I did want to govern this kingdom. A child like myself might have as good a chance of governing a country as the tyrants who had ruled before. But I so badly needed you and Yin His! I couldn't bear to think that you might have left us forever. I wanted you for my counsellor, Master. Oh, Yin Hsi, I'm so sorry! Please forgive me!"

Big tears started to trickle down the new ruler's cheeks. She hid her face in her hands, while Yuan Song came across to the massive Throne and gave her slim shoulder a friendly squeeze.

"Hahaha!" laughed Lao Tzu. "See, there has been no real harm done, Jade Fish, and I enjoyed poor Ning Mei's embarrassment. But are you really serious about wishing to rule this country? Governing anything is not to be undertaken lightly, you know."

"I've never been more serious in my life," sobbed the girl. "I want to become a wise and worthy ruler. You know, when I was living in the Border Town, I sometimes used to sneak away sometimes and sit at the back of the Magistrate's Court and that is where I started to dream.

"I never thought I would ever get the chance, but my dream was of creating a better world. I wanted to be able to give children like me a better chance in life. Then, I was given this opportunity and I wished to put into practice some of what you told us on our journey. But I see now that I was beginning to do just what my aunt, Zhou Ting, was doing. Using my power to get my own way."

She wiped her eyes, looking so sad and small in the huge, ornate throne, surrounded by the beautiful, green-blue peacock feathers and all the painted finery.

"Ah, my poor, dear Jade Fish," said the Master sympathetically. "Don't you remember that reading of the *I Ching* you told me about? You drew the Hexagram *Fu* or 'The Return'. The aspect was positive. It said you would be amongst friends who would support you, but there was a warning about not straying from the Path as things developed. Do you not remember that?"

"I do remember," said the girl, hanging her head.

"Perhaps you acted from good motives," said Lao Tzu gently. "It's hard to let people go and to say goodbye. You didn't have your parents there to help you when you were small, which may have left you feeling more dependent on someone like Yin Hsi or myself."

"I didn't want to see you go!" cried Jade Fish. "I still want you to stay. Please, would you not remain here to be our First Counsellor?"

Lao Tzu shook his great head so that his big ears flapped vigorously.

"I'm old and tired," he said, his eyes twinkling mischievously. "I've written all that needs to be said, and even that is far too much! Yin Hsi will look after the Texts and they will be there for you or anybody else to consult. I wish now to pursue a path of silence and emptiness in the wilderness out to the west. My old water buffalo, Shuïniù, is waiting at Yin Hsi's home. We will both go together."

"What should I do, then, Master?" asked the girl, still wiping her eyes with a small cloth Yin Hsi had passed to her. "Is it wrong for me to try to rule a country? I'm not educated and I have little experience."

"Ruling a country, as I told the Cook, is just like cooking a small fish. Can you remember that?" asked the Master. "You, I know, can cook fish very well, so ruling should not be beyond you! Rulers should all be like children, for children have the right instincts in general. Education and experience have *never* guaranteed good government."

"Then how *should* I govern?" asked the girl anxiously.

"Oh, dear!," sighed the Master. "Yin Hsi, my friend, what shall we tell our poor, heartbroken Jade Fish? When has there *ever* been good government? When have rulers ever been able to govern themselves first?

"Jade Fish, I have written it out, but there is never any harm done in repeating good advice. Do not seek to do too much. Rulers who interfere and work terribly hard, end up chasing shadows. It is easily said and much harder to put into practice, but the best rulers lead from *behind* not in front. They remember that for every advance there must be a retreat; for every movement there must be stillness; for every light there is also darkness. Yin goes with yang. They are not opposed. A coin must have two sides."

"I shall try to remember this, Master," murmured the girl, still full of sadness. "Yin Hsi, may I be allowed to have the scrolls copied?"

"Your Highness, they will be at my home waiting for you," answered the tall Gatekeeper with a smile. "You have only to send for them, though my wife and I would be most honoured if you wished to come in person."

The girl smiled back and brushed her wet eyes with the back of her hand.

"I will come in person if I'm still just Jade Fish to you and your wife, sir," she said. "When I come to visit you and when I visit the shepherds, I shall not forget my past nor who I really am. I would like my parents and their friends to visit you also.

"But... but, I shall miss you so much, my Master!" she said, turning to the vast old man, her eyes beginning to fill again.

8   The following morning Lao Tzu made his formal goodbyes for a second time, and then he and Yin Hsi prepared to be escorted back to the Border Town by Ling Hu and the palace guards. This time they would be travelling alone, for the Magistrate and his wife had already set off towards the town, having left before dawn under cover of the silvery darkness

Before this, however, the Master and Jade Fish went out early to practise their exercises for one last time in front of the lake. It was a quiet moment together and a happy one, where all was smooth and unhurried. Some of the girl's heartache was eased, and as she shared in the old man's inner serenity she knew that his peace would also never leave her. He would always be there and his words and writings would be there too, in her heart, forever.

Together they stood on the dew-soaked lawns in the grey dawn. The swans still had their heads entwined in sleep. The male peacocks were only just spreading their colourful fans and beginning to try out an occasional screech to greet the coming day. There was a faint blush in the sky beyond the line of distant mountains. Lao Tzu and Jade Fish, however, concentrated not on the view but on their breathing. Their feet and arms were balanced in pushing and parrying, as they formed circles which had no beginnings and no endings. Their hands described full circles that were both old and young, male and female, yin and yang.

Everything was in perfect harmony.

9   A lone bird chirruped cheerfully in the high trees lining the lakeshore.

He sang to the world that there is no beginning and there is no ending.

He announced that there are arrivals in life and there are departures.

As Lao Tzu and Yin Hsi were climbing into their carriage, Fan Lian, beautiful and charming as ever, suddenly arrived in another carriage from the east, unannounced, with her best friend, Li Po, the equally lovely grand-daughter of Mu Ju. The two women were accompanied by Bien Jin, who had asked to escort them on his father's white stallion. Bien Jin's mother and his young sister were also with them.

"News travels fast these days," Fan Lian said, hugging her daughter once more. "I wanted so badly to see you again and, of course, I had to meet this Lao Tzu, whom you talked about so much. Bien Jin also wishes to make his acquaintance. And his widowed mother has been so keen to meet you, my dearest one."

The Emissary's widow, a gentle woman with sad eyes, stepped from the carriage and was presented by Bien Jin to Jade Fish, who returned her deep bow with a shy bob and nod of welcome. Bien Jin's mother could not help glancing up at her handsome son proudly, the sadness of her eyes melting into happiness as she saw the two young people shyly exchanging warm smiles.

Introductions were then made, compliments were paid and Yuan Song was called over to meet the party, handsome in his red leather armour. Jade Fish's jade green eyes flashed with joy. Instead of one mother, she now discovered she had two. Li Po had short black hair cut straight across her forehead, framing her pretty face. She was strong and well spoken, with enchanting, dark eyes that lit up when she laughed, which was often. Fan Lian and she made a happy pair together.

The girl's father, Yuan Song, too, seemed to flourish in his role as Regent and protector. He and Ling Hu had good ideas for developing a more responsible army for the defence and protection of the kingdom without, however, having to resort to violence. They wanted to outline their plans the next day, they said. Yuan Song declared, moreover, that on this important day all business should be set aside and the occasion should be marked with a special feast.

The Master was humbly begged, therefore, to delay his departure for just one more day. Jade Fish looked anxious as she saw Lao Tzu hesitate, but it was only to ask the Gatekeeper if he would not object to staying on a day longer.

Yin Hsi was, indeed, willing to delay their departure, so all was well.

The old Nurse was overjoyed to find her grand-daughter once more and it was at once agreed that Mu Ju would return home with Li Po and Fan Lian, to be properly looked after at their school and to share in their lives.

That evening a state banquet was ordered, the first to celebrate the reign of Princess Jade Fish, or Yu Yù as she wished to be known.

The Cook joyfully set to work with her new team of palace staff, preparing a feast that would be fit for this grand event. To the surprise of only a few, Mu Ju the old Nurse, the Cook, the Gardener, other servants and the Herbalist were all included in the gathering, which seemed more like a family dinner than a state banquet. Not very many of the new courtiers, however, were invited, though all the former bandits were there. Lao Tzu was happy with the style of the evening. He said that he preferred informality.

Soon, everybody in the palace dining hall was eating and talking and laughing. They all chatted to their neighbours or called cheerfully across the table, helping each other to the succulent dishes and the various drinks. Of course, they ate fish. Not a small fish, but many golden carp giants, reared in the palace ponds.

Lau Tzu's great, rumbling guffaws could be heard even down in the kitchens. Court etiquette seemed to have been put to one side, for that evening at least. Jade Fish recounted some of her adventures; her father blushed at certain memories; and Ling Hu was much praised, along with the Herbalist, for saving the life of the Peacock Princess. There seemed to be so much to talk about and to laugh over.

"So, my daughter, Princess Jade Fish, or Yu Yù," said Fan Lian towards the end of the evening, "might we now ask your illustrious Master to share with us some of his secrets about how a country might be wisely governed and about how we might all achieve happiness in our lives?"

The idea was a popular one and everybody looked about the banqueting hall for the enormous old man with the huge ears. It was dark outside and the hall was lit by beautiful coloured lanterns. Had the Master, not just a minute ago it seemed, been telling them such strange and amusing stories, full of riddling wisdom? Had he not made everybody think themselves truly important and specially honoured, when he spoke to them? And had his plump and wrinkled old eyes not twinkled with dark mischief, when he was asked if he really intended crossing over to the forbidden lands of the Qin and beyond?

The guests looked around the hall anxiously. Would the Gatekeeper perhaps know where the Master had gone? Yin Hsi, however, was nowhere to be found. And Ling Hu, who might have had some idea, was not there either. This was most strange. There had been no leave-taking, no final salutations, no last minute directions or counselling.

But Jade Fish's head was bowed lower than before, as Bien Jin's mother spoke softly with her. The girl's face was wet.

For Lao Tzu, her Master, had mysteriously vanished.

Which person has more than enough and gives it to everybody?
It is the one who knows of Tao.
Therefore the truly wise work without recognition.
Achievements are gained without any fuss or need for recognition.
The wisest do not show off their knowledge.

(**Tao Tê Ching** - The Classic of the Way and Its Virtue - LXXVII)

End of Book One

Names Book One

Bài Mâo – Mu Ju's white cat

Bien Manchu – The Emissary

Bien Xing – his wife

Bien Jin – the Emissary's son

Chan Shui – The Wise Woman

Zhou Hin – Zhou Ting's husband and consort

Zhou Ting – former ruler and queen of the Peacock Throne

Fan Lian – the sister of Zhou Hin and mother of Jade Fish

Göu – the dog

Jade Fish - Kitchen Girl, later Princess Yu Yù

Lao Tzu – the Master

Li Po – Mu Ju's granddaughter and servant and friend of Fan Lian

Ling Hu – young former bandit

Liu Bao – Fan Lian's assumed name

Mu Ju – the old Nurse

Nang Soo Chong – the Herbalist

Ning Mei – the Magistrate's wife

Ning Wen – the Magistrate

Pao Shen – the Shepherds' dog

Shuïniù – the black Water Buffalo

Tan Kuo – the Jade Cutter

Tan Lan – The Jade Cutter's wife

Wei Shan – the elderly shepherd

Wei Shu – his wife

Yin Hsi – the Gatekeeper

Yin Nuan – his wife - **Yin Chao** (their little boy)

Yuan Song – robber baron and father of Jade Fish

2 pretty serving girls, twin sisters at the tea shop (Sun Ju and Sun Shafen)

My thanks particularly to Sophie Vermander,
our dear friend, who has been able so proficient
and generous with her time in overseeing
the layout of this book and the succeeding
volumes of the trilogy.

P. S.

Cover: shutterstock_1945324501

Drawings: Paddy Salmon

ISBN: 9798386796853

Independently published

Printed in Great Britain
by Amazon

23804236R00116